# IN TED WE TRUST

*and other short stories*

Jon Rowland

In Ted We Trust and other short stories



Cover design by Anne Currie.

Jon Rowland
@jon_rowland

Gravitational Press
@GravPress

First Printing: July 2019

ISBN-9781070135731

To Alison for supporting me when I was writing and
Anne for encouraging me when I wasn't.

# Contents

# The Tree

In the fifty years the human race had known we were not alone in the universe, there had been no more sign of our elusive neighbours. Not the tiniest hint of who they were, where they were located, or whether they were still alive. At the time, that one momentous encounter had been enough to reinvigorate the world's interest in space and drive humanity's expansion into the solar system. Sadly, the event itself was fading from the mass consciousness – now little more than a historical footnote.

So much so, when the con flashed up a broadcast notification of an NTO event from SkyGuard, Rhona MacKenzie had to flick it open to see what the three-letter code referred to. It was the first time she'd not recognised a code since she was a rookie pilot nine years earlier.

She read the missive and tried to call Phil on the ship-wide – he'd get a kick out of this, she was sure.

He answered after a minute, "Something wrong, Mac?"

"You busy?" she asked.

"Just finished deploying the collection rig. Contact looks solid. Waiting for the results of the sampler. Assuming this rock's the same as the last twenty, then we should be ready to grind in about an hour. So, I've got a little time. What's up?"

"SkyGuard just notified us that they're tracking a non-terrestrial object."

"You mean... aliens?"

Rhona laughed. "Let's not get carried away. It just means they've spotted something they can't immediately explain."

"I'm coming up there!"

"Wait, Phil, there's no point, it's only..." He was already gone.

It was a long walk from the business end of the ship up to the cockpit, so Rhona was surprised when her out-of-breath engineer staggered in through the hatch only ten minutes later. He must have run the whole way – probably the most exercise he'd had in years.

"Any more news?" he asked, between lungfuls of air.

Phil had recently turned sixty and was usually the epitome of a no-nonsense, seen-it-all space veteran, but Rhona now saw the restored sparkle of youthful excitement in his eyes. Despite the sweat running down into his beard, he looked twenty years younger.

She shook her head with a wry grin. "No, sorry. It

was just an informational. I already told you everything I know. There wasn't much point you coming up here."

He looked a bit disappointed. "Didn't they say where it is, or what it is, or anything?"

"Nope. And I doubt they will. If it really is something, then they'll not be broadcasting anything until they've investigated more. It was probably an automated message."

He collapsed into the other chair, the sparkle fading slightly.

Rhona felt sorry for him. He looked like a little boy who'd had his toy skimmer taken away. "You remember the first one?" she asked him.

He looked up at her, some of the energy returning. "Course I do! I was nine. My folks were worried about what it all might mean, but to a lad who loved science fiction, it was exciting."

"You really thought that? I mean, it was just space junk, wasn't it?"

Phil rolled his eyes. "You kids these days have got no imagination!"

Noticed by chance during a calibration run of the Webb Space Telescope, The Triangle (as it became known) raced through the solar system in a matter of weeks. It was constructed from a mesh of metal bars forming what looked to be the corner of a structure. The opposite ends showed significant blast damage, fuelling speculation it had been thrown off into space as part of a significant explosion.

In an unprecedented global effort, a prototype Chinese ZX-S shuttle was retrofitted for unmanned flight and launched within a week on a one-way intercept course to get a better look at the object.

"My parents let me stay up all night watching the pictures as they arrived, right up until the shuttle fell out of range. I remember the moment they found the writing like it was yesterday. Just amazing! The President has that picture on his wall in the Oval Office, you know."

Rhona nodded, "Yeah, I knew that. Shame they never managed to translate it."

"It was the fact there was someone out there who could write it that was important. It probably says 'do not step here' or something, but that's not the point. *That's* what made me want to get out here among the stars. The idea that somewhere out there, there's someone looking back at us." He sighed. "Of course, the time since has been a bit of a let-down. But maybe that's about to change."

It was interesting to see Phil like this; it was a whole different side to him, but Rhona didn't understand the motivation. She'd come to space to get away from people; she liked the quiet. The last thing she wanted was aliens invading her space – figuratively, or literally.

She was about to say as much to Phil when the

con flashed up an incoming communications request. She shared a frown with him – it was rare for anyone to use audio out here. Even with Earth in a favourable location like it was now, the one-way lag was over fifteen minutes.

She opened a channel. "This is the Asteroid Mining Corporation vessel *Vanity Fair*, pilot Rhona MacKenzie responding. We are standing by for your message."

She turned back to Phil. "I wonder what's up. Well, nothing to do now but wait. You'd best get back to that grinder. Those rocks aren't going to mine themselves. I'll let you know what happens."

He nodded. "Aye. Be sure to let me know if we're being overrun by little green men."

Just over thirty minutes later the response arrived. "Hey, Mac. This is Reggie at SkyGuard control. I'm relaying a message from the ISA. Stand by." What the hell did the ISA want with her? When the message continued, the voice was different – older, more serious, with a slight accent.

"Good afternoon, Ms. MacKenzie. My name is Doctor Dev Chopra, I'm the operations director at the International Space Agency." Rhona sat up straighter in her chair, even though he couldn't see her. She knew who he was – the best-known name at the ISA, she'd seen him on vid streams countless times.

"As you'll have seen from the informational that

went out earlier today, we have detected an object of unknown origin travelling towards the Sun, roughly on an intercept course with the Earth. The object appears to be spherical, about ten kilometres across, but its most interesting property is that it is slowing down."

Well, that was curious – an object that size should have been speeding up under the influence of the Sun's gravity. Rhona could see what all the fuss was about, but that didn't explain why the ISA director had sent her a personal message about it.

He continued. "We are going to scramble a science team out of SkyGuard to intercept it, but the best-case simulations have them reaching it in about two weeks, assuming it maintains its current direction and deceleration. And... well, not to put too fine a point on it, we're a bit worried about missing the boat."

Rhona got a sinking feeling – suddenly she knew where this was going. *Little green men indeed.*

"You're the closest ship to the object's current path, and we think you can intercept it in about two days. We've spoken with your superiors at AMC, and they've given the go-ahead for you to undertake a detour and get some early close-up observations. Understand that all we're asking you to do is pull up alongside it and transmit images back to us. You won't even have to get that close. Obviously, though, we can't force you to do this. We understand it's well outside your job description – although I'm told you are an excellent pilot."

A bit of flattery to seal the deal? Like she had a choice. Phil would kill her if she said no. Worse, it would be a PR disaster for AMC and she'd be out of a job, pronto.

"So, I'm asking you, for the advancement of the human race, if you can do this for us, on this potentially historic day."

She scowled at the con. *You can stop with the arm-twisting – I've already decided to do it.*

△△△

Forty-seven hours later, having abandoned a perfectly good coupling with asteroid 6732, the *Vanity Fair* slid in alongside the NTO and matched velocity.

Phil had been on tenterhooks the whole way and had stayed away from the screens until the ship was as close as possible so he could get the best reveal. So now he was rather deflated. "It's another bloody asteroid!"

"I mean, it's a pretty impressive one – bigger than anything we've ever mined," pointed out Rhona, trying to get him to see the bright side, although she had to agree with the gist of his assessment. His enthusiasm had been infectious, and she felt equally let down.

The furore had lost its head of steam in the intervening two days – the object had stopped slowing down, leading to speculation it had previously hit debris in its path, and there was now no danger to Earth – it was going to pass by harmlessly.

Rhona pointed the all scopes at the rock and set up the feed to stream back to SkyGuard. The plan was to gradually adjust their relative position, so they could send back pictures of all sides – in particular the bits that weren't visible from home.

It wasn't much different to her normal job of manoeuvring the ship into position amongst the asteroids in the belt. Except in those cases Phil had things to do other than staring over her shoulder and demanding she zoom into every blotch and depression on the rock's surface in case it was evidence of, well, anything. Rhona tried to be tolerant, but much more of this and she would have to kick him out of the cockpit for a bit, so she could make progress with her mystery novel in peace.

The book was getting to a good bit when Phil piped up again, "Holy shit! Look! Mac, look!"

She sighed, she hated to do this, but he was driving her nuts. "Phil, I know this is kinda your thing, but I... holy cow!" Her eyes had drifted to the screens and so she was now staring at the same picture as Phil. She grabbed the control stick and zoomed in on the image. "But that's... impossible."

Phil was grinning ear to ear. "Never in doubt!"

Hard to make out clearly in the darkness, but unmistakable nonetheless, growing from the surface of the otherwise featureless asteroid was a large tree. A trunk, branches, twigs, and even what looked a bit like leaves in places, although it was hard to be sure.

Rhona managed to snap herself out of slack-jawed mode and opened a channel back to SkyGuard. "Control, you'll, uh, have seen the latest images. Please advise." She paused and then added a timecode and coordinate reference in case they somehow missed what she was referring to.

Phil was still poring over the images. "What do you reckon? Broken off from a planet? Artificially grown there? Either way, it's evidence of life!"

"Maybe," Rhona admitted, trying to temper her own response to the revelation. "It's a shape. It could be anything. Just because it looks like a tree from this angle, doesn't mean..."

"Oh, come on! You don't believe that. That, right there, is evidence there's life out there. We're going to be famous!"

*Great*, thought Rhona. *Just what I need.*

The response from Chopra was professional, but Rhona could hear the renewed energy in his voice. Only this time no amount of flattery was going to convince her to do his bidding.

"They want us to go down there?" asked Phil, his eyes wide.

"Yeah, and I told them where to go."

"What?! But..."

"No buts, Phil. It's ridiculously dangerous, we're not trained for it, and the ship's not designed to couple with an asteroid this size anyway."

"She could handle it."

"That's not the point. Everyone's being impatient – the science research ship can get a proper look when it gets here. We are not risking our lives for the sake of a couple of weeks."

"You... I..." It was pretty much the first time she'd seem him properly angry. With visible effort, he managed to stop himself saying anything he'd regret. He turned and stormed off towards the stern.

Rhona took a deep breath. She hadn't expected him to take it that badly. Part of her was as curious as he was, but she had a responsibility for the ship and for their lives. Short of a direct order from the AMC director she wasn't going to put all that in jeopardy to appease some scientist, no matter how famous he was.

The direct order, in effect, came an hour later. The director was genial, but firm. "Rhona. Can I call you Rhona? The world is watching. Two weeks of waiting for answers would be very poor publicity for AMC. It's in everyone's best interests to push ahead with this operation." Everyone's best interests? Everyone who wants to keep their job he meant. Subtle.

Phil, his anger forgotten, deployed the grapples while Rhona prepped the EVA suits. She was half-hoping the surface of the asteroid would be too hard to achieve attachment, but it reacted like normal rock. After that, it took minimal manoeuvring to pivot the *Fair* so her stern faced the barren surface allowing Phil to reel them in.

The couplers secured the ship to the asteroid's surface about two miles from the tree – they'd not wanted to risk getting too close. The ship was never designed to fully land on an asteroid, so Rhona kept the engines ticking over, maintaining separation, with the grapples holding the rear of the ship close enough for them to disembark.

Rhona surveyed the scene. "You sure this is going to hold?"

"Aye. No problem, as long as there's no unexpected acceleration."

"Let's hope there isn't then. Come on, let's get this over with." She pulled on her helmet, waited for him to do the same, and flushed the airlock.

Stepping out onto the rocky surface of the asteroid was strange – the gravity was much weaker, even than that generated by the ship, to the extent that it was more like operating in zero-G. The exception was there was a definite *down* that Rhona's balance mechanisms didn't seem to think was any more interesting than any other direction, despite her eyes telling her otherwise. It was disorienting.

Phil grabbed her arm to help steady her. "You OK?" He was much more used to operating in unusual gravity than she was, safe up in the cockpit most of the time.

"Yeah. Thanks." She was acutely aware this was all going out on the feed and she was grateful he'd prevented her from christening the alien surface with a faceplant. She made sure the little retractable spikes on her boots were working – locking her to the surface while stationary. Once she felt secure, she took in the view before them. "It's smoother than I expected," she commented.

The rock was rugged, but not in an extreme way. Yellowish-grey peaks and troughs were scattered across the vista, but none of them high or steep. The path to the tree would be straightforward. It was located roughly at the backward-most point relative to the object's trajectory, protected from the impacts of any debris in the planetoid's path. She wondered if there had been other trees, lost to time and collisions. Was this solitary one here by design or coincidence?

The surveying floodlights of the *Vanity Fair* were powerful, but, shaded from the distant sun as they were, it still got oppressively dark as they half-walked, half-floated their way away from the airlock towards the tree structure. Rhona felt a chill – she liked to be alone, she liked the quiet of space, but this was something else. Even with Phil beside her, this place felt desolate.

The tree became clearer as they got closer and the lights on their suits started to penetrate the darkness more. The most important news was it still looked like a tree. There'd been no trick caused by the light or angles. About the size and shape of a large oak, it rose incongruously up out of the featureless plain.

Phil whistled. "Well, ain't that something."

Rhona played her light over it, taking it in. It certainly was something. But that something wasn't a tree. At least, not in the traditional – Earth – sense.

There was no bark. The surface was a dark grey colour, covered with a delicate pattern of faint lines running up the length of the trunk and along the branches. The spread of the branches was irregular, with large dense clusters of smaller forks in some directions and nothing but empty space in others. The elements she'd thought might be leaves were the most different – they were more like flexible spines crammed in their thousands onto the twigs. Again, they were uneven. Only a small number of offshoots were coated in the spines, the rest bare.

One thing was clear: this was not a naturally occurring structure. She had no idea what it was – a statue commemorating a historical event? the engine powering the asteroid through space? – whatever the truth, this was unmistakably alien.

Phil stepped nearer, playing his light over the formation, trying to get a better look.

"Careful, don't get too close!" warned Rhona. She suddenly had the feeling she was trespassing.

As Phil moved his light around, a glint caught her eye. "Wait – go back... down a bit... yes, there – see that?"

"Yeah, I think so. It looks... newer."

One of the many branches was a lighter grey than those around it, and even had a bit of a shine to it. Phil was right; it looked newer than the rest. Was this tree growing? She walked around the whole thing, casting illumination on every offshoot. The one she'd noticed was the only part which had the different look. If it was growing, why would it be doing it in only one place? Compared to many of the other branches, this one was also fairly bare, with only a few twig-like extensions at its end, and none of the spiny leaves.

"Do you think that's significant?" he queried.

"Hard to say, but it's definitely interesting." The puzzle had made her momentary trepidation fade.

A moment later, the conundrum was put to one side as their attention was taken by a visual treat. Rhona had noticed on the charts SkyGuard had sent over that the asteroid's path through the solar system happened to pass close to many of the planets – aided by several being in rough alignment at the moment.

As they stared through the branches of the tree, behind it, Mars rose majestically into view, climbing up from the curved horizon.

Rhona gasped. "Wow. That's quite the view! Almost makes all this worth it."

They watched together as Mars rose overhead, and then shrank into the distance as the object continued on its rapid fly-by.

"I guess we've probably done about as much as we can, given we don't have any of the right tools to measure much of anything else," said Phil, sounding a bit disappointed, but resigned.

But Rhona was once again staring up into the branches. "There's a new branch!" she exclaimed. She focussed her light on it, and, sure enough, at the end of the new growth, there was now one more small fork. "That last one definitely wasn't there before. It just appeared! Damn – I wish I'd kept looking at it. We missed it growing. Stupid Mars!"

Phil chuckled. "You'll have to write a letter of complaint to the ISA. *Mars in inconvenient location, please consider changing.* Looks like even the tree doesn't approve – that new twig is pointing right at it."

It was true; the growth pointed directly at the red planet as it receded into the distance. "Huh, weird coincidence!"

They waited a while, but there was no sign of further activity from the tree, so they returned to the ship to write up notes of what they'd seen to complement the streamed images. Rhona hit confirm to send it off to the powers-that-be and turned in for some well-earned sleep.

She'd hoped new instructions in the morning would say they were done, but the word from Chopra was to stay put while the ISA did more analysis of the information they had sent. Rhona found, to her surprise, she wasn't disappointed – the tree was still a mystery, and she did love a good one of those.

In the subsequent week while they waited, the *Vanity Fair* riding like a parasite on the asteroid's back, Rhona visited the tree twice more. It remained resolute in not giving anything more away.

The dull wait at least gave her a chance to catch up on more reading. Phil passed the time doing maintenance on the grinders, and other mechanical tinkering.

The following morning, they finally got good news – the science vessel was, at last, on its way to relieve them, and would be there soon – the asteroid was, after all, approaching the vicinity of Earth.

△ △ △

Rhona awoke on the final morning feeling bittersweet – on one hand she was glad to be getting back to normality, but she felt like there were unanswered questions here. Remembering the great view of Mars, she did some calculations and worked out there was time for another show before the other ship arrived.

She stopped by engineering to offer Phil the chance to join her for the spectacle, "You want to come and watch the Earth rise?" But he was busy prepping the ship for decoupling from the rock, so she pulled on her EVA suit and headed out onto the surface by herself for the final time.

As was now customary, she checked over the tree for any sign of new growth. There was none, so she positioned herself so she had a good angle from which to see both the tree's silhouette and the imminent rise of the Earth over the horizon.

This time the angle and the lighting were exactly right. As the Earth rose, she saw it: the tree grew! It was the same as the last addition – a small extra fork at the end of the shinier branch, next to the one that had sprouted when they encountered Mars. And this one pointed right at the Earth.

Gears began to turn in Rhona's head, connecting dots, forming theories. The new branch was related to the planet. She was sure of that now. She played her light over the whole area, counting the offshoots, the separations between them. Four twigs, two thicker well-spaced ones, two smaller ones closer together – the Mars and Earth ones as she'd started thinking of them – all reaching out from the main bough in the same plane.

She tried to visualise the current position of the planets from the last time she looked at the charts, overlaying the path of the asteroid – past Neptune, past Jupiter, then Mars and now Earth.

It made sense, but if she was right, then that would mean... With the Earth now overhead, she looked back at its associated twig. *Yes!* The new growth still pointed towards her home – it had bent around to follow the new relative direction of the Earth as it passed by.

"My god," said Rhona, not quite believing it could be right, but sure of it all the same. "It's mapping the solar system!"

She stared at the tree in awe. This wasn't merely alien. There was intelligence here. Was this a computer? An alien device sent out to explore the stars and record what it found? Or was the tree itself an intelligent lifeform?

The tree loomed over her with new significance and she realised she'd been so distracted by the revelations of what it was doing in this solar system, she'd missed the magnitude of what she'd worked out. There was a whole tree here. Did each division of the trunk represent a galaxy? Each branch a star? How far had it travelled? It had mapped the location of thousands of planets. The data here would be a goldmine for astronomers.

She looked back at the little twig representing her home – and that of nine billion other humans –

it was humbling. One tiny speck amongst so many others.

As she stared at it, something else changed. More growth. The Earth twig was sprouting leaves! Thousands of the prickly spines soon coated its surface – one of only a few on the whole tree with such a covering.

And suddenly she knew what it meant. Her eyes widened. Life! The spines were indicating the planet was *populated*. That wasn't news of Earth, but there were other spiny branches. Our elusive neighbours now had an address!

Rhona's head was spinning. This was world-changing news and she'd figured it out. Beaten the scientists. So much for not being famous. *Damn*.

Still, it wasn't worth much if she didn't tell someone about it. She turned and headed back in the direction of the ship, opening a channel to Phil at the same time.

"Hey Phil, can you patch me through to Chopra. Or SkyGuard." Anyone who would listen!

"Now? I'm in the middle of prepping the couplers to detach." He sounded a bit annoyed.

"Yes, now! And you'll want to hear this. I've got amazing news!"

"Really? All right, gimme a second."

To her surprise, a few minutes later she got a live audio feed in her ear from Chopra. The science vessel must have been close, and he was aboard.

"Miss MacKenzie, I understand from your engineer you have some exciting news to relay?"

The *Fair* was coming into view up ahead. She should have waited until she was inside and set up a video link to talk to him properly, but she wanted to tell *someone*, and she knew he'd appreciate it.

"Yes, that's right! I think I've figured out..."

At that moment, there was an almighty lurch beneath her feet! Rhona instinctively sank into a squatting position for additional stability, but the boots' spikes already held her safely to the surface. The ground seemed to be moving under her. There was also a terrible noise in her ear – the sound of metal being put under tremendous strain. It took her a moment to realise it came from Phil's mic, still hooked into the feed.

*Oh no!* She raised her head in horror just in time to see the *Vanity Fair* floating away, her coupling arms having lost their tenuous grip on the rocks under the strain of the asteroid's sudden movement.

"Mac! Tell me you're on board!" came Phil's panicked voice over the channel.

"I'm not! I'm not!" she replied, fighting back her own panic. Panic was the last thing she needed – a calm head was imperative in these situations. If only her racing heart would realise that.

"Shit! All right. Hang on. Let me get up to the cockpit and see if I can swing her round and pick you up." Of course, while Phil was qualified to manoeuvre the *Fair*, he was nowhere near the pilot she was. Worse, Rhona feared it was already too late. The asteroid was accelerating away from the ship. The distance growing by the second. If that continued, it was unlikely Phil would even be able to catch up – it wasn't a fast ship.

△ △ △

After what seemed like an age, but was probably only an hour or so, the sensation of being dragged along by a rumbling giant faded, and she felt able to stand up again. The rock had stopped accelerating.

She turned to get her bearings and, to her shock, the Earth was now a rapidly receding dot in the distance. She was moving fast now. Light glinted off another object – Chopra's ship. It looked like they had turned to try to pursue; Phil must have explained what had happened.

Rhona tried to contact him – let him know she was still alive. Still OK. But the channel was dead. Out of range. The suit's radio was low power – never intended to operate away from the immediate vicinity of the ship. She couldn't contact Phil, or Chopra, or anyone.

The feeling of desolation and aloneness she'd first had on stepping foot on the rock was returning. She was in big trouble.

More time passed as the adrenalin from the

shock coalesced into a lump of cold terror sitting in Rhona's stomach. How could they reach her before her air ran out? Could they even reach her at all given how fast the rock was now moving? Could her suit withstand the extra radiation as they passed closer to the sun? There were a hundred ways for her to die.

Worse, she'd never even had the chance to relay her revelations about the tree's purpose. Maybe they'd work it out from the videos, but it didn't seem obvious unless you were looking at things in the right way – realised the rock was visiting the planets to perform scans.

*Wait!* That was it. The path of the asteroid wasn't random. It had only visited four planets so far. She knew what it was doing – why it had accelerated. It was going to slingshot around the Sun and back out in a new direction from which it could intercept the remaining planets in the solar system. They didn't need to catch her. All they needed was a way to intercept her path.

Not that that did her any good. Unless they reached the same conclusion, she had no way to communicate her realisation.

"Miss MacKenzie?" The sudden voice in her ear startled her. It was Chopra. "We are focussing a narrow-beam boosted signal on your location. You won't be able to talk back as your radio doesn't have the transmission power, but we also have commandeered one of our orbital telescopes to get a look at you, so we can see you. If you can hear me, please give us a thumbs up!"

Her saviour. Maybe. At least there was hope. She gave a thumbs up and held it for several minutes facing in the direction of Earth – there'd be a delay on the images and the radio messages, so she wanted to make damn sure they knew she'd received the message.

Once she was certain they must have seen her, she turned her attention to working out how to convey the other information she needed to get across. She tried to remember those star charts again, and hence the likely path of her strange steed.

"Acknowledged. We can see you can hear us. We are working on the problem. This craft does not have enough acceleration potential to catch up, but we are exploring other options. Please bear with us. From the information we have, we believe your suit should have power and hence oxygen generation and hydration for several more days." She checked the read-out; she had time.

There was nothing she could make a mark with. The surface of the rock was smooth. There was only one option for trying to communicate. She tried it, feeling ridiculous. Hopefully, they'd be able to make it out given the relative angle of the telescope, and wouldn't think she'd lost her marbles and was trying to do the dance from YMCA. It took a few moments to work out how best to represent the letters, and it was even harder to twist her arms around in the bulky EVA suit, but she thought she'd managed to do a decent enough job.

A few minutes later, she got notification of success. "Hi Rhona, we think you're trying to spell out the word V-E-N-U-S – Venus. Can you give us a thumbs up if that's right?" The voice's owner didn't bother to introduce himself, but she was happy to give him a double thumbs-up nonetheless. Message received. Now she had to hope Chopra and his team were smart enough to figure out what it meant.

It took them two hours before they came back to her. Chopra himself again this time. "Miss MacKenzie, we are interpreting your message to mean you believe the asteroid will pass close by Venus, presumably with the intention that fact might offer us a way to intercept you, even if we cannot chase down your current trajectory. Our calculations show the object will need to slow down substantially as it passes the Sun to achieve a slingshot around to the correct vector. I'm not sure how you could know this, but if we've interpreted you correctly please signal with the customary thumbs-up."

She would be getting tiny in Earth's scopes by this point, but she did her best gesticulating to indicate they were spot on.

This time it was three hours before they got back to her, and the signal was getting sketchy by this point. Chopra was hard to make out, but not so much she couldn't pick up the tone of his voice. There was not good news.

"Miss MacKenzie. Rhona. We have looked at the simulations. Even with the advance notice of your position you've provided, we do not have any spacecraft close enough to reach you by the time you get there. I am so sorry. A rescue just doesn't look possible. I feel responsible. Had I not asked you to go down to the surface, this never would have happened."

*You* are *responsible!* thought Rhona, anger only one of the several emotions rushing through her in a confusing mess. How could this be possible? All these years after The Triangle had revitalised the push to the stars, space travel was commonplace. If rich tourists could go ice-climbing on Ganymede, how could there be no ships close enough to help her?

All seemed lost, but only a few minutes later, a familiar voice came in over the increasingly shaky connection. "Mac, it's Phil. I'm not giving up on you just yet! I've got an idea. I'm talking to the boffins. Bear with us while...." His voice faded into static. She was out of range. Or the Sun's proximity was generating too much interference. Either way, she suspected she wouldn't hear from them again until she was on the far side of the star. Could Phil, of all people, have thought of a solution the team of scientists had missed? She clung to that thought as she settled in for a cold few days of lonely travel.

△ △ △

As the asteroid passed Mercury and approached the Sun, Rhona, fearful of the additional radiation, took shelter behind a steep rise in the rocky surface. There was nothing now to do but wait. Without the radio contact, the isolation set in again. Even if Phil did have a solution, what if *she* were wrong. The rock could continue on at this pace and fly out of the solar system too fast for anyone to even ever speak to her again.

However, as the light grew brighter with proximity, Rhona felt herself pressed into the ground as deceleration kicked in. She had been right! The slower-moving object was affected more by the star's gravity field, pulled into more of a slingshot, eventually shooting out the other side in the direction of Venus. She hoped.

As the rock turned with the help of the Sun, the tree's branches shifted over her head, adjusting to maintain their directions, remaining pointing at the planets they had mapped out – further confirmation her theory was on the money.

It seemed like an eon passed before her radio crackled back to life. "Mac? I'm hoping you can hear me. We no longer have an angle to see you, so I'm just going to have to go on what they're telling me – that this signal should be able to get through to you by now." Phil's voice again. "We have a plan. But, it's a little tricky."

Tricky she could deal with. Any plan was better than no plan.

Phil continued, "We have a ship that can get to you." *Yes!* "But it's not very manoeuvrable. We don't want to get too close to the asteroid in case there is a collision and we lose our one chance to get you. So – and this is the dicey part – we need you to, er, get off the rock."

Get *off*? It wasn't like she could ring the bell and ask to be dropped off at the next stop.

"The gravity is really low and the scientists reckon if you can make a good jump from the highest rise you can see, then you should make escape velocity so you can get clear. We need you to do it as close to Venus as you can, and then we can get the ship to pick you up."

Rhona's heart was racing now. She understood the physics in principle, but to try to leap off a solid object so she'd be floating in space – on purpose – seemed deeply counter-intuitive.

It was still a decent wait before she reached Venus, and Phil's message was repeated several times on the way, making sure she'd received it. By the time the yellowish planet rose over the horizon, Rhona had had plenty of time to psych herself up to the task ahead. The fact her air was getting low provided an extra incentive too.

As the tree sprouted another branch behind her, recording Venus's existence, Rhona summoned all her strength and pushed upwards from the asteroid's surface.

With the tiny gravity of the rock, the leap sent her floating up way above the ground. It was disorienting but gave her a fantastic view of the churning atmosphere of the inhospitable nearby planet. And of something else. Sunlight glinting off its hull, there was a ship – her ride. She smiled as she recognised it. Phil must have given those young scientists a history lesson. The Chinese ZX-S shuttle had fallen into a wide orbit around the Sun after its interception of The Triangle half a century ago. An orbit not far from Venus as it turned out. With power still left in her nuclear reactor and the remote-piloting systems used back then still working, Phil's brainwave had saved her life. The shuttle would have air and water enough to keep her alive.

If she could reach it. She realised with dismay the asteroid was getting bigger again beneath her. She'd not got clear; the gravity well was too strong. *No!* She needed to start higher, get further clear of the planetoid's mass before jumping off. She scanned the surface as she gently settled back onto it. It was too flat, too uniform. The ridge she'd used was the highest point she could see.

*Wait!* The highest point on the ground, but not *the* highest point. She looked up at the tree. It rose far above her. It would give her enough of an edge, she was sure.

Climbing the tree was awkward in the EVA suit, but the low gravity made it possible. She pulled herself up the trunk and then along the branches until she was near the top.

Taking a deep breath, she once again pushed off towards the shuttle. This time it felt better, she was moving faster. She was going to make it.

Relief ran through her as she took one last look down at the asteroid. She had much to tell about what she'd learned, but she wondered if the rock's true nature or origin would ever be known.

As the tree's branches grew smaller, her eyes sought out the small set of offshoots that represented this solar system. One small part of a huge universe, but not an empty one. Then she gasped as her gaze fell on a feature of the tree she'd not noticed until now. Much to tell indeed.

With only a small amount of adjustment in the shuttle's position, she was able to intercept it and make it to the airlock. Inside was cramped and uncomfortable – space for human occupants replaced with the retrofitted automatic systems. But there was power, and air and water to last her until the real rescue party reached her. She was safe.

Once out of the EVA suit, she activated the

communications system and reached out.

"This is Rhona MacKenzie. Is there anyone out there?"

It took a while to get a response – she was still far away – but when it came, it was Phil's welcome voice.

"Mac! Thank God! Are you OK?"

She smiled and thought back to the last thing she'd seen as she'd floated away from the asteroid. Venus's newly grown tree branch covered in tiny spiked leaves. All that time staring at the stars wondering who was out there, and there was life in the most unlikely of places, right in our own backyard.

"It's good to hear your voice, Phil! Yes, I'm pretty good, considering. Listen, I've got lots to tell you. You'll like it. It's about little green men...."

# Construction

## *Watchers I*

Bob worked in construction. Or at least that's what he used to tell people. It was true his work involved building things, but it wasn't houses, or fences, or roads. Bob built alibis.

Tonight's client was the usual pasty-faced, nervous sort. Shifty glances, pulling at his collar, the works. He seemed reluctant, as they always did, to tell Bob what it was he needed an alibi for. This was, of course, crucial to constructing a plausible trail of evidence to defer suspicion.

Bob put on his most reassuring face, one that had been well honed over the years. "Mr. Schaeffer, it's quite all right. I guarantee absolute confidentiality. My job would be pointless and impossible without it. I have a reputation to protect after all."

It would take a few more minutes; a few more supportive comments and then: "I killed my boss!" The confession.

Bob nodded sagely. Run-of-the-mill. "Has the

body been found yet?"

Schaeffer raised his head, stopped studying his knees. "Oh god, yes. This was fifteen years ago!"

Not so run-of-the-mill after all. "Mr. Schaeffer, don't you think, that if you've got away with it for the last fifteen years, you're fairly safe?"

The man, clearly suffering, shook his head. "No."

Bob was becoming exasperated. "And why would that be?"

"Because I went to the police station this morning and confessed...." The head hung down once more.

"Good grief," said Bob.

"They didn't believe me. And then... And then I changed my mind." Schaeffer looked up again, frowning, maybe about to cry.

"Try to stay calm, sir. Forgive my ignorance, but I still fail to see the problem. You confessed; they didn't believe you. Sounds like the case is closed and you're home free." Normally first consults were free. Bob was rapidly deciding to charge this nutcase through the nose for wasting his time.

Schaeffer sighed. "No, you don't understand. Tomorrow, the Watchers are going to resurrect him!"

Bob gasped. "You've got to be kidding! That's a one in a billion chance – you can't be that unlucky!" Suddenly the man's dour demeanour made more sense.

"He'll identify me straight away. I'm screwed. Especially after what I did this morning. I don't know what I was thinking! I just felt so guilty."

This case had now become something to grab Bob's interest: a challenge. "You're sure it's him?"

The client nodded. "It was on the news this morning."

"All right, Mr. Schaeffer, let's get some details...."

An hour later, Bob still sat at his desk, staring down at the notes he'd taken, mulling it all over. This was unprecedented: a first-hand account of a murder; the ultimate witness. Bob had to come up with the mother of all cover stories. Not easy. But doable, surely? Fifteen years was a long time. Any other witnesses would have faded, rusty memories. All there was to back up the facts were records. Records could be doctored.

After much deliberation, he had a plan. Simple, elegant. A masterpiece. It was late, but with the resurrection the next day, there was no time to waste. He started simple: hacked a few systems, tweaked a few files, altered a few details.

With the harder stuff he had to call in a few favours. People were unimpressed to be woken up at the late hour. He ended up using up some significant IOUs he'd been owed for a long time, but he didn't mind. This was his life's work; the ultimate cover. It had to be perfect.

Eventually, as the sun started to rise, he'd done it. There was just one last loose end to take care of. Bob got up from his desk, stretched, yawned, picked up his coat, and went to complete the scam.

On the tram across town, the resurrection ceremony was showing on the screens. The crowd watched with the morbid fascination that always surrounded these things. He wondered what this guy, seemingly normal, had done to warrant resurrection. It was rare for anyone who'd died in the last century to be brought back. To get the call within fifteen years was almost unprecedented. Bob had got lucky – without this he'd never have had the chance to practise his ultimate art.

When the Watchers had first arrived, their huge ships floating in the sky, there'd been panic and fear. Over time it became clear their claims of only being interested in observing humanity and learning about our culture were true, and the strange new status quo became accepted. While the Watchers remained inscrutable, they had eventually gained popularity. They won us over first with their slow drip-feed of technological upgrades for the betterment of our world, and then with the bizarre, impossible practice of bringing people back from the dead. Creepy but fun. Albert Einstein's Friday night chat show is wildly popular.

The latest resurrection was well under way. The

cameras zoomed in as the dull mound of clay was shaped by invisible hands, taking form, gaining life.

As Schaeffer's boss opened his eyes again they went wide. "Oh my god! I was murdered!"

The watching masses gasped in unison, and the police approached. Then to everyone's surprise, they handcuffed the resurrected man and arrested him!

Bob got off the tram, grinning. It was all going perfectly. He walked the short distance to his client's house, and knocked.

Schaeffer opened the door looking shocked. The end of the ceremony showing on the screen behind him. "You did it!" he said, amazed, ushering Bob into the room. "It's impossible! You're a genius!"

Bob smiled, satisfied. "Yes. Some of my best work I think. Most pleasing."

Schaeffer sat down, relieved. "How on earth did you do it?"

"I just turned things around. The one way they wouldn't believe his accusations was if they thought he was himself a murderer. All I needed to do was change a few records. People are all too willing to believe what their computers tell them."

"Brilliant! So, he's a wanted murderer now? How did he die?"

"Oh, he committed suicide out of guilt for his crime. Of course, I wanted to change as few details as possible, so he still had to have been found dead at the same location."

Schaeffer nodded. "You're worth every penny of your fee! Out of interest, who did you have him kill?"

"Well, again, details tied you to the scene of the crime, so I had him kill you."

That took a moment to register. "What? But how is that possible? I mean, I'm here!"

Bob pulled out his gun and fired a single shot. "No, Mr. Schaeffer, you're not."

The bullet was a special kind – one of the handy science upgrades the Watchers had provided. It was only a moment before the body started to dissolve. Bob turned and started his walk back to the tram station.

No loose ends.

# The Dealer

I eye my fellow travellers with suspicion as I stand in the ticket line. Any one of them could be the Dealer. Few of them are the sort of people you would want to meet in a dark alley. Our destination is no holiday resort; there are no first-class seats, no space stewards to cater to your every need, and no travel insurance.

There are about twenty people in the line in total. The transport ship holds about twice that, plus a generous cargo space. The only other time I went out to Hessar, I travelled in a stinking heap I doubted was space-worthy, along with a barnyard's worth of farm animals and an old man with halitosis. The ship this time is larger and runs to a scheduled timetable. Still, I'd rather be heading for the sunny beaches of Raya on a luxury liner.

I reach the desk and give the unenthusiastic clerk my name. I reserved my ticket ahead of time. I need not have bothered given the low turn-out.

After some confusion we locate my booking under *Kat Saviour*. How my name mutated to that from *Frank Taylor* is a mystery, but with ticket in hand I make for the dock.

I board the ship and head to the seating area. There are no assigned seats, just a communal lounge. To my surprise, it is clean and comfortably furnished. There's not much in the way of entertainment, though we will only be in the lounge area for about ten hours of the three-day flight. The rest of it will take place while we are securely strapped into grav couches, safe from the ferocious accelerations and decelerations and oblivious to the world.

Sitting in the lounge gives me a good opportunity to eye up the rest of the passengers. If my source is right, one of them is the Dealer, but knowing which one will be impossible for the moment. I just have to bide my time and take opportunities to glean more information as they arise.

I'm an agent with the Drug Enforcement Agency, but the Dealer isn't smuggling traditional drugs. My target is the galaxy's most cunning purveyor of medical nanites.

The theory of using nanotech for medicine was sound; the nanites could perform the most intricate of tasks without the trauma of invasive surgery. In reality, millions of microscopic, interacting robots in the bloodstream formed a system with such complexity that chaos theory intervened and made the whole thing too unpredictable. Tiny errors in cell manipulation would lead to cancers, strange new diseases, or worse. The risks were assessed as being too great to patients.

Research continued, but the government stepped in and outlawed the use of nanites until they could be made safe. Inevitably, something so useful with a relatively low risk attached to it immediately moved underground. That meant underqualified engineers were manufacturing poor quality nanites and causing even more risks and disasters in their application.

The authorities were able to stamp out the trade on Earth. It was initially less of a problem in the colonies; most of them are mining outposts, too poor to afford the expensive equipment required to manufacture the nanites. Eventually, supply and demand met, and a solution was found – the export of illegal nanites from Earth. That's where I come in. I've been working on this case for several months. The supply line is still small. We must act fast to shut it down before it gains critical mass.

All the evidence points to one individual being responsible for over eighty per cent of all the nanites being smuggled out to the colonies. I'm closer than ever to tracking him down. I say 'him' based only on the balance of probabilities and my own gut. In fact, it could be anyone: man or woman, adult or child. The Dealer is so hard to catch because he uses the nanites himself to change his appearance – cosmetic adjustment is one of the more reliable functions they can perform. He will never appear twice in the same guise in the same place. That is why, sitting studying faces, I have no idea which of the people scattered about the lounge could be him.

I've been in this situation before, but never so well informed. This time I have what promises to be a full itinerary for his trip: visiting three colonies and then heading back to Earth. Hopefully, I'll be able to find a single individual out of the twenty or so current options who takes the route I'm expecting. Then it will be a case of waiting until I can catch him in the act. There is always the possibility he will change his appearance along the way, but I'll be on the look-out for that. I suspect the grav couches are the best place for him to make that sort of change – several hours of isolation with no risk of being disturbed.

We've been under way less than an hour when the captain asks us to enter our grav couches ready for acceleration up to travelling velocity. The grav couches are unimpressive looking things for what they do. I always think they look a lot like plastic coffins, which is less than reassuring. The couches work by surrounding your entire body with the most disgusting gloop I have ever seen. It then hardens, keeping you safe from the enormous g-forces. The whole experience is rather claustrophobic, which is why you also get a shot to put you to sleep for the duration. I take one last look at everyone before I head to my couch, trying to commit their faces to memory so I can notice any changes when we wake up. Confident I will spot any differences, I climb naked into the cold goo, seal the lid and am soon sound asleep.

Waking up in a grav couch can be a disturbing experience, especially if it is one of the older ones that do not open automatically. You can lie there trapped and encrusted in solidified gloop for several minutes before someone comes to let you out. Fortunately for me the grav couches on this transport are automatic. Regardless, the experience of peeling off the hardened goo is never a pleasant one.

The Hessar system is a go-slow zone. We still have several hours of transit before we come into dock, so there is no risk of my quarry slipping away before I can check for a change of appearance. As the passengers slowly return to the lounge one by one, I carefully tick each one off on my mental list. Unfortunately, everyone is accounted for and there are no new faces. I find this disheartening. So far, I have no confirmation the Dealer is even on this transport.

Hessar is one of the older mining colonies. A decade ago it was thriving, but now with most of the planet's resources extracted it has fallen into disrepair and is a hang-out for the dregs of humanity. The wind blows the musty air in my face as I leave the dock. According to the itinerary I have for the Dealer, he is only scheduled to spend a few hours here before moving on to another colony. Given I have no leads as to which of the passengers he might be, there is nothing to do but bide my time and try and match a face on the outgoing transport with one I have already seen on the way in.

I head towards the centre of town from the dock, hoping to find a pay-by-the-hour room where I can freshen up. As I walk down the main street, I catch my reflection in one of the store windows. One thing strikes me: it is not me.

I turn and face the image full on, not believing what I'm seeing. The man in the window is my build, my height, but looks twenty years older than my thirty-five: hair greying at the temples, worry-lines. The nose is wider and the eyes blue instead of green. I look like someone else entirely.

There can only be one explanation. Someone has injected me with nanites and they have done their work while I was in the grav couch. The only person who would want to do such a thing is the Dealer. That means I'm at an extra disadvantage:

the Dealer is onto me. Why would he change my appearance? As a warning? To give me a face he can recognise more easily? To give me a face that will get me in trouble here on Hessar? I will have to be extra careful who I run into from now on.

My mind turns back to the job in hand. At least I now know the Dealer is here on Hessar. I know he was one of the faces on the transport. And I know it is likely he is here to conduct business. I force myself to become more alert and take in more detail about the surroundings. There could be clues anywhere.

As I pass an alley, I hear a commotion. Investigating further, but staying in the shadows, I see two large men kicking and punching a third man. As an officer of the law it is my duty to protect the innocent, but I'm in no mood to get a beating, and I suspect there are not many innocents in this area anyway.

The two men decide they are finished, and the victim is thrown up against the wall in a sorry state.

"Don't come back here again with your nanite shit!" warns one of the men as he walks away.

Now this obviously piques my interest. It seems unlikely the man against the wall could be the Dealer. He would have an arranged appointment and is too smart to get into this sort of trouble. The man is probably a just a user, but I'm keen to find out exactly what went on here. It may offer a lead on my target.

I move out from the shadows and walk down the alley, ignoring the man slumped against the wall as best I can. He's whimpering quietly. He'll live, but he won't be a pretty face.

The building the two large men have disappeared into is an entertainment establishment of a particular type. Hardly a surprise – there's not much else to do out here in the back end of the galaxy except shovel rock and screw.

I walk in the door, following in the footsteps of the two men. Inside the décor is fading, but presentable. I find the two of them guarding the inner entrance. I nod at them and walk on into the main part of the building. They ignore me.

Inside is a bar, an empty stage and doors off into a number of rooms. The barman glances up at me. He looks a seasoned fellow. Probably the owner or manager, and not just there to serve drinks.

"Two drink minimum," he states flatly. "Anything else we can discuss after that."

I sit down at the bar. "Scotch, straight up." He gets me the drink and charges me three times what you would pay for a fine single malt. It tastes like paint thinner.

"I notice you had a little trouble just now," I say, trying to sound nonchalant.

He grunts. “Yeah, joker comes in here and injects one of my girls with nanites. He's lucky to be alive if you ask me.”

I raise an eyebrow. “Really? What happened exactly?”

“Stories come with a three-drink minimum.”

I shrug. “Hit me with a double.”

So, I get the story. “Happens from time to time. Doesn't matter that I've got the best selection of girls on Hessar. Idiots come in here armed with a syringe stuffed with nanites thinking they will do a bit of customisation on their lady of choice. Just for that extra kick. Of course, they're all cheap, so they get the nastiest stuff, real low grade. There's no way I want my girls with that stuff in their blood. Got myself a filter in back. Gonna have to sort Lucy out in a minute. She's still in tears back there.”

“Interesting,” is all I say. I’m not convinced this is going to turn into a useful lead after all. I’m sure the guy in the street won’t have got the nanites in question from the Dealer directly, probably second- or third-hand on the local black market. Even if he did, he is in no state to tell me anything.

Something else occurs to me though. I have the Dealer's nanites in my blood. It’s possible he could be using them to track me. Finding a man with a filter might be a stroke of luck.

"Gonna have to go sort out Lucy now," says the bartender, interrupting my thoughts. "Back in a few."

"Hey, wait." I call after him. "I was wondering, d'you think it would be possible for me to use that filter too?" I don't think it's worth explaining my exact circumstances. He would either say yes or no, I doubt he would care beyond that.

He stops in his tracks and turns back to look at me, eyes narrowed. After several seconds he nods. "Yeah, OK. Come on back."

Lucy is in a bad way. We find her huddled in the corner, tears rolling down her face, arms wrapped around her knees.

"Come on honey," says the barman gently, "let's get those things out of you."

She looks up at him and smiles slightly. It's only when she gets up I realise exactly why the guy in the street got such a beating. Lucy, who I presume started out the day as an attractive young woman, is now a lop-sided mess. The left half of her body is athletic and tall with short brown hair. The right half is a short full-figured blonde. She stumbles across the room awkwardly, her legs different lengths. The filter will do nothing for her current condition, but will remove the risk of the nanites malfunctioning further and causing more damage. Nothing short of surgery or higher-quality nanites will fix her up.

The filter works by using an electromagnetic field to attract all the nanites to a single point in the body and then extracts them from there into a syringe.

The barman does Lucy first. She seems happier when the procedure is over and immediately goes back to her room to catch up on sleep. The barman throws the vial of nanites that have been collected into the rubbish and turns to me.

"You next."

The needle from the filter stings a bit, but is not too uncomfortable. The whole procedure takes about ten minutes, and when it's over he collects the vial of nanites and puts it in his pocket. This surprises me until it occurs to me maybe he thinks they can be reprogrammed to help Lucy out of her fix. I know I should make him destroy them, but he has helped me out and I'm primarily interested in the Dealer, so I say nothing.

I'm half expecting a bill for the use of the filter, but the barman nods at me with a hint of a smile and says, "Be seeing ya, then."

I nod, realising that is my cue to leave, and I head back out through the bar hoping the two bouncers are not going to follow me out and teach me a lesson too. Fortunately, nothing of the sort happens, so I wander back out onto the better populated main street and consider what to do next.

I only have a few hours before the next transport leaves, headed for Polack II, so I decide the best use of my time is probably to head back to the dock and keep an eye out for any familiar faces. The picture on my ID doesn't match the face on my head, but I'm confident security will be so lax out here no one will even bother to check if I have a ticket, so it won't be a problem.

The dock is deserted when I get there. The outgoing transport has not even arrived, and the waiting lounge has no one more exciting than a janitor sweeping the floor. I settle down into the most comfortable seat I can find and wait.

No one else turns up for another half an hour, and when they do it's no one I recognise from the first transport. The route from Hessar to Polack II is rather off the beaten path. With only ten minutes left before the transport is due to leave, there are still only ten people in the lounge.

As they call the gate, she walks in. A young woman, maybe nineteen or twenty, with longish dark hair and a rather sullen expression. A face I recognise from the first transport. In a way I'm pleased: if I only have one lead, then I won't have to make a possibly incorrect decision about who to follow. On the other hand, if the Dealer is on to me, would he (or she) be so obvious as to appear unchanged on the second leg of the journey? If not, the Dealer could be any one of the fresh faces I have encountered in the lounge.

I decide I might as well follow the only possible lead I have and stop worrying about it. If the Dealer is someone other than the young woman, I'm back to square one anyway and can gain no advantage by sitting around doing nothing on Polack II.

Nevertheless, if the girl is the Dealer, I will be surprised. To travel among the mining colonies in that body – weak, attractive and female – seems foolhardy at best. I do not doubt the Dealer will be armed and able to defend him- or herself, but to me, it seems like you would do best to stack the odds as much in your favour as possible.

As the captain calls for us to enter our grav couches, I realise I've neglected to memorise any of the new faces on the transport in my preoccupation with the woman. I curse under my breath and take a last look around, trying to commit as many to memory as possible as they go to their couch chambers.

I'm still fuming at myself as I let the protective fluid surround me. If the Dealer is not the girl, then I might miss an important mid-flight change that would alert me to his presence. Polack II has an open shipping channel all the way up to the planetary orbit, so I will have a much shorter period of time to check for changes in the other passengers before we have to disembark.

The lid of the grav couch comes up, and I notice

it straightaway this time. Either the dealer has got me again, or the barman's filter did not do the trick – probably the latter. The skin on my arm is much darker than before, and I soon discover it matches the rest of me. My body is still my own, but my face is once again changed. It makes sense: a change of apparent race is much easier and cheaper to achieve with nanites than a whole body resculpting. Cursing, I realise examining my change has delayed me in getting out of the grav couch chamber. By the time I've dressed, we're already in dock and most people have left the ship.

I put my lapse down to grogginess from the nanites' effects, which can be tiring. I move as quickly as possible out onto the dock, trying catch sight of my only lead: the woman.

To my relief, I see her exiting the building and hurry after, attempting to look inconspicuous. Satisfied I have her near enough not to lose her and far enough not to raise suspicion, I settle back down to a gentle stroll.

I'm relieved when she walks away from the seedier end of town. Polack II is still going strong as a mining colony and as such is rather more salubrious than Hessar, but there are still areas I'd rather avoid.

Her destination is an unmarked building without windows. I position myself outside with a clear view of the main entrance and the side door down the nearby alley. I want to observe the place for a while before I go in.

Noticing a comms point in the wall next to where I'm standing, I decide to be a good citizen and warn the barman on Hessar his filter is faulty. He seemed to be a decent enough sort, despite his profession, and I'm keen to avoid his employees getting sick through faulty machinery. I don't have a name, but I know the street address of his establishment, so that will have to do. I send the missive and stand around in the cold for the next half hour.

There's no sign of activity and finally I get bored and risk going into the building. Inside, I'm surprised to find myself in a well-lit waiting room populated by a pregnant woman reading a book, and a rather stern-looking receptionist. The place is a medical clinic. There's no sign of the girl I followed here, but suddenly the chances of her being the Dealer seem slim. This looks like a dead-end.

I'm about to apologise to the receptionist and claim I've taken a wrong turn when she looks up at me and asks, "You the guy from Hank?"

This throws me, and my mind starts racing. Two possibilities hit me. Either Hank is the barman from Hessar and has called ahead to arrange a second attempt at filtering my nanites – unlikely as all hell, but possible – or the Dealer has set me up with this face to be recognised for some purpose. Either way, I decide it's probably a good idea to answer in the affirmative and see where it leads. If it turns out 'Hank' sent me here to be given a lethal injection – well, it will end my day on a downer.

She takes me along a corridor and into one of the examination rooms. We pass two more pregnant women on the way, and I realise this must specifically be an antenatal clinic.

"Thought you'd never get here. We have quite a few anxious patients who'll be glad to hear you made it."

I've no idea what she is talking about, but I'm used to winging it by now. I even have a better disguise than usual for undercover work. "I'm sorry to have kept you waiting."

She shrugs and says, "Well, let's get on with it." To my surprise she reaches into one of the desk drawers and pulls out a nanite filter. Was I right? She is doing a favour for the barman on Hessar – agreeing to refilter my blood. On the other hand, her words make no sense to me and don't really conform to that theory. I'm still certain the Dealer is involved in all this somewhere, but I'm getting the sinking feeling he is simply too smart for me and I'm going to be running in circles for the whole trip.

Still, there's nothing I can do about it now. I

press the filter's needle into my skin and set the extraction process going. The waste jar slowly fills, and, when it is finished, the woman takes it from me and puts it in the desk drawer along with the filter.

She seems satisfied. “Thanks. Next time use the side-entrance though.” She directs me that way and soon I’m back out on the street, still a little bewildered by the experience.

I hang around for a few more minutes, keeping an eye out for the girl I followed in here in the first place. I’m not convinced she is a key part of the equation any more, but I know she must have played a role. I can’t believe it’s a coincidence I ended up in the right building for whatever it was I just did for ‘Hank’. There’s no sign of her, so I abandon the lead and move on.

The transport to Long Shores does not leave until the morning, so I move up into the ‘posh’ end of town and find a motel with a room for the night. It’s not somewhere I would ever bring my mother but will do for a bed.

After showering, I stare at my face in the mirror for a long time. It is not a face I recognise. I wonder if it belongs to a real person, or if my appearance is merely recognisable enough for the needs of the Dealer’s plan.

There is more going on here than meets the eye, but I’m still in the dark. It’s infuriating. I feel like the Dealer is taunting me, pulling faces in dark corners behind my back. Hoping a good night's sleep will help me arrange my thoughts, I jump into bed and am out like a light as soon as my head touches the pillow.

I sleep long and deep, my body taking its chance to recover from the trauma of the nanite modifications. After I've had a shower and grabbed something disgusting resembling a bagel to eat, I go to the dock.

There is only an hour left before the transport to Long Shores is due to leave – an altogether more appealing location. It too used to be a mining colony, twenty years ago, but its long beaches and pleasant climate have meant it has evolved into a tourist resort. It might even rival Raya one day. I don't expect the transport to be anything fancy, though; there are direct transports from Earth to Long Shores. I'm well off the tourist route, approaching from the opposite direction.

I can see the transport already in dock as I approach. It is big and newer than the two I have already travelled on, but is still no luxury liner. I guess most of the space is for cargo – shipping raw materials to build new hotels to meet the increasing demand.

Before I reach the terminal, I get a surprise. The girl I followed yesterday passes me in the street. Just for the briefest of moments, she makes eye-contact and mouths, "Thank you." She seems much happier than she did on the transport the day before. She disappears into the crowd before I can intercept her. What was she thanking me for?

My brain whirrs into action, the thoughts it has percolated throughout the night are slowly linked together by this event, and I add two and two and get six.

The Dealer is bloody clever, I will give him that. Abortion has been illegal on Earth since scientists developed a way to turn fertility on and off at will with a simple injection. Not everyone can afford that treatment though. Nanites, programmed correctly, provide a non-invasive way to terminate a pregnancy. And what better place to do that under the radar than an ante-natal clinic on an out-of-the-way mining colony.

What happened here is now clear. The woman extracted the nanites from me and used them, reprogrammed, to get her patients, including the girl I followed, out of their undesirable situations.

It all starts to fall into place: the bottom line is I have been used. The Dealer injected me with a batch of nanites at some point, either on the first transport or even before I left Earth. They activate, change my appearance and through a series of seeming coincidences, I deliver a batch first to the barman on Hessar and then to the woman on Polack II. All the time I think he is toying with me, he is using me as a delivery van. How could I be so stupid? There is no need for him to come out here and risk his neck. No, just let Frank Taylor be your mule!

I curse repeatedly as I walk the final steps up to the terminal building. No doubt there is another appointment waiting for me on Long Shores. An apparently harmless series of events will lead me to the right place, and maybe a third person will offer to filter my blood. Well, I won't fall for it this time. I know exactly where to go when I reach Long Shores. I'll get rid of his damn nanites and then I will track the bastard down once and for all.

To my surprise and relief, I find the nanites have been at work and I'm once again myself when I reach Long Shores, although I have picked up a nice tan. There is logic to this: Long Shores, being a tourist resort, has more stringent entry requirements than the more remote mining colonies. I doubt I would have got in with an ID card picture that did not match my face. The sun is warm and the people altogether more pleasant, and I feel much better as I put my plan into action.

The university on Long Shores is a campus affair, with buildings done up to look ancient and majestic. In fact, it is only ten years old. A favourite study location for those who also enjoy the beach. The one fact I know that brings me to it now is it has an active nanotechnology faculty. Nanotech is still an advancing field, but it is hard to get the licence for a lot of research areas at old Earth universities. So, the most forward-thinking minds head out to the colonies and enjoy their research in the laxer judicial atmosphere.

Unfortunately for me, it's Sunday and there are not many people about. I finally find a person who I think can help in a basement lab of an otherwise deserted building. I know I have the right place because the young man in question is peering into a cage containing a creature which is a bizarre mix of cat and dog.

I clear my throat to get his attention. He looks up. He is in his mid-twenties, has a shock of dirty blond hair of medium length pushed behind his ears, and is wearing a lab coat splattered with what I suspect is pizza sauce.

"Hey man, didn't see ya there. Was just checking up on my lab partner here." I must look shocked, because he immediately breaks into a toothy grin. "Don't worry, man, I'm just yanking yer chain!"

I ponder my luck at finding the only comedic Californian nanotechnologist on the planet, but I shrug it off. I have more important things to worry about, and my choice of scientist is limited.

I return his grin. "Interesting pet."

His grin stays put, "Yeah. Used to be a mouse."

I suspect the irony is not lost on him, but I don't

pursue it.

"Help ya?" he asks. He most certainly can.

I explain a version of my predicament that manages to leave out most of the sticky details. The key point is I have nanites in my blood I would like to get rid of and he has the equipment to let me do that. He's not sure if he should help me, but I promise him the precious nanites for use in his research if he does. This offering convinces him, and he runs me through a full body scan.

The results take over half an hour to process, and I sit sipping over-hot, bitter black coffee while I wait. Finally, the man, whose name I have discovered is Mike, emerges from the inner lab.

He looks up at me. "Interesting stuff, man. Your whole body is infested with nanites, and not just common ones either – top of the range, multifrequency, high durability ones."

Multifrequency explains why the previous filtrations failed to pull out all of the nanites. I suspect each customer had their filter set to the relevant frequency to extract the nanites they had paid for. I was just a walking flesh and blood envelope for their deliveries.

"So, can you get them out?" I ask, without much hope.

"Can try." And he does, but with only partial success.

"Sorry, man. My filter doesn't have the

frequency range to pick them all out. Got maybe fifty per cent, but the really clever ones are still left in there."

I nod. "There's nothing else you can do?"

He considers for a moment. "Well, I can extract the core program and maybe even tap into the instruction set and make adjustments. That any use?"

It is. With the core program, I can work out exactly what the Dealer's plans for me are. I can see what my rendezvous on Long Shores was supposed to be, maybe come at it from a less obvious angle and pick up some useful information. I can possibly also trace the program back to its starting point and learn where it was the Dealer first injected me.

I give Mike the go-ahead to try and extract the nanites' core program. He puts me through yet another piece of equipment that queries each nanite molecule in turn and pieces together the instruction set. The results are encouraging.

"Here we go, man. Got a full list of all the high-level instructions to be carried out by the nanites. Looks like you've been through it!"

I nod. "You could say that. Can you transfer it to my tablet?"

"Sure thing." He sends it over, and I sit down to read it. It's all there. The dates, the delivery locations and the frequencies of the filters to be used to extract the correctly programmed nanites, and the programs to run to give me the correct appearance for each job. I feel thoroughly used.

I flick to the end to see what my intended location on Long Shores is meant to be, and I can't help letting out a short, ironic laugh when I see the address of this lab and the exact frequency ranges that Mike has extracted for me. I start to say something, but stop myself. The Dealer has outsmarted me, well and truly. There is no use dwelling on it. At least I have valuable evidence, so my trip has not been a total waste.

The real shock comes when I go back to the first page to try to determine where and when the Dealer first injected me with this batch of nanites. I slump into my chair, my breath catching in my throat. The first nanite instruction on the page states:

*Assume identity 48 (Frank Taylor, DEA)*

My mind races. There is only one explanation. The truth is too impossible for me to comprehend, yet undeniable: I am the Dealer.

How can that be? How can I be chasing myself? How can I be the Dealer without knowing I am the Dealer? It makes sense, of course. The subtle ploy of a genius mind – my own genius mind. How can you catch a criminal if the criminal does not know he is a criminal and the only person chasing him is himself?

My mind is spinning, but I know what I have to do. My own plan has backfired on me this time. Regardless of the bizarre details of the situation, there is one fact that is inescapable: I have caught the Dealer. My long hours have finally paid off, and my quarry is within my grasp. It means turning myself in. I feel myself peering over the edge of insanity, teetering on the brink. I pull myself together. There is one more thing I must do before I head back to Earth, one more thing I must know, and I know the man to help me.

“Mike?” He looks up from where he is storing off the nanites he has extracted from me, and probably paid well for in an indirect and complicated way. “Can you do a system reset? Force the nanites to revert this body to its original form?”

He thinks for a moment and then says, “Probably. If they're using the usual base instruction set, which they seem to be, should be easy.”

“Excellent. Can you set it to trigger in four hours?” He can.

The advantage of Long Shores being a more mainstream destination for Earth travellers is that the IDs are all checked before you get on the transport. So, if I arrive on Earth looking like someone else, I'll be able to disembark with no problems.

My mind is still in utter confusion, grappling to hold on to the facts as I climb into my grav couch for the trip back to Earth. In a few hours the nanites will have done their final work and I will know the Dealer's, my, true identity.

As it turns out, I was wrong all along. The Dealer is a woman, after all. It is an unusual experience to wake up a member of the opposite sex – but no stranger than realising you are your own nemesis. I'm proud of how I'm dealing with the weirdest day of my life. In hindsight, it makes sense the Dealer is a woman given the specific uses the nanites I delivered were being put to. I feel a moment's doubt – the Dealer is distributing high-quality nanites which are being used to help people. The implications of prosecuting the Dealer for my own well-being are less than attractive. Could I see a way to cover this up? No! I will do my job. This justification and self-preservation is exactly what the Dealer was hoping for. I will not give her the satisfaction of manipulating me again.

It is late when we dock. I head straight home. I'll go into the office to turn myself in as soon as it opens in the morning. The rogue nanites are still in my system, but that's a secondary concern.

I'm dog-tired. The much more severe change of becoming a woman – losing a lot of body weight –

has taken much more out of me than the previous, less major changes.

I leave my tablet with the all-important breakdown of the nanite program on my desk, so I don't forget the key piece of evidence in the morning, and head to bed for a night of troubled dreams.

△ △ △

I get up at dawn and head straight into town. I know the boss will be in early. I clutch the tablet tightly in my hand, excited by its contents. There is hardly anyone around when I get into the building, but I see Marcy sitting on reception looking tired and bored.

"I need to talk to the chief," I tell her.

She looks me up and down. "Kinda early. Go on up."

Upstairs there is no one around, but the chief's office is lit up. I knock and go in.

The chief is in his late fifties and running to fat, but he is a smart guy and I have nothing but respect for him. He peers up at me through the wispy steam coming off his coffee. "What do you want at this time in the morning?" he asks.

"I've got a solid lead on the Dealer," I say, fingering the tablet.

"Is that so?" His eyes drop to the tablet in my

right hand and I pass it to him. He reads the screen. He regards me again and ponders for a moment.

"All right, Frank. Take the trip. But this itinerary better be more accurate than the wild-goose-chase I approved last month, or it's your ass, understand?"

I nod. "Thanks, chief."

This time I will get the Dealer. I can feel it in my blood.

# Small Gods

Henry, Supreme Being of Life and Evolution, stood in the men's room of the Woodsville town hall and examined his reflection. Imposing? He straightened his tie. It would have to do. Judith would kill him if she knew he'd come straight into work, but he'd been fretting about it for the whole duration of the trip. He hardly liked to leave the office for a mere decade; the century or so he'd been away this time was a bit more than he believed his minions could handle in his absence.

He tried to calm himself. It would all be fine. After all, the town itself still looked much the same – it was comforting to be home – and he'd left the Department in Tom's capable hands. The Supreme Being of Sex and Reproduction was a level-headed guy; he'd have kept things under control.

After smoothing his suit one last time, Henry turned and headed up the stairs to greet the team.

On the journey home from the New Project, he'd thought hard about how to make a good entrance. He hadn't been able to come to a firm conclusion. He wanted to take immediate charge but didn't want them to be unhappy he had returned. A fine balance was needed.

In the end, he just opened the door out onto the office floor and walked in. To his relief, everything looked much the same. It took a few moments before anyone spotted him, at which point there was much clattering of plates and straightening of backs.

Katie, Demigod of Leaf-symmetry, stood up, beaming too broadly. “Sir! You're back! How was the trip? Can I get you a coffee?”

Henry scanned the room and put his finger on what was missing. “Where's Tom?”

The question met only a roomful of blank stares and nervous smiles.

“Well?”

“He, uh, quit, sir,” said Katie, looking like she wished she sat further from the door.

Henry blinked. “I beg your pardon?”

“It's true,” another voice confirmed. “About thirty years ago.”

“Quit? But... what happened?”

“Said he'd had enough, sir. Said he was sick of doing all this day in, day out, and never getting a single bit of worship.”

“Worship?”

“Yeah, he said you'd think that after doing a job for a species for a billion years you'd get a little gratitude.”

Henry was incredulous. This was unheard of. No

one ever quit, especially not an old stalwart like Tom. "But that's what all the churches are for..."

"Yeah, but Tom said he wanted personal recognition," explained Katie, warming to her subject. "Not just abstract generic worship to some non-existent figurehead."

Henry's mind started to race. This was a disaster. All these demigods with no supervision for decades! Who knew what they might have done?

Trying to gather himself, Henry surveyed the group of expectant faces. He took a deep breath.

"Right, I want a full report of *everything* that's happened since I've been gone! Reports from everyone on my desk in an hour. Oh, and Frank?" he added, turning to his chief engineer, "I used a new single-sexed tripedal dominant species for the New Project. Works much better. Look at my notes and work something up on how hard it would be to back-apply that here. By tomorrow, please."

△ △ △

Ed had been so keen to impress the boss with his report, he'd dashed down to the Department of Time and borrowed a couple of extra hours so he could really polish it.

At first when he'd received the request to see Henry in his office the next morning, he was sure his extra work had paid off: the boss wanted to commend him on his great new ideas and the advances they'd generated.

Now, having seen the look on Katie's face on her exit from a similar meeting, he wasn't so sure.

Katie had picked up the abandoned reins of Tom's job when he walked out – someone had to. She'd had the splendid idea to make sex a fun thing to do, rather than only for reproduction. This had been a wild success with the general populace, especially the humans.

What could Henry possibly have said to make her look so shell-shocked?

Finally, the waiting was over and Ed was called into Henry's office. Henry's face was searching, showing a disappointing lack of recognition but otherwise unreadable.

"Ed, is it?" asked Henry.

"Yes, sir."

"And you are Demigod of Bumblebees, correct?"

Ed nodded. "Yes. Well, actually, it's the principles behind their ability to fly that require divine input."

Henry waved a hand dismissively. "Yes, yes, fine." He reached into a file and pulled out a large photograph and held it up for Ed to see. "Then I'm a little confused, that being the case, as to what *this* is doing in your report."

Ed half-frowned, half-smiled, confused – was this heading toward a promotion, or not?

"They call them aeroplanes," he said, proudly.

Henry frowned. "So I understand."

Ed pushed on, "Same underlying principles at work there, you see, sir. I figured, if bees can fly and birds and all, then why not let the dominant species in on the idea."

Henry was silent for a long time. Then, leaning forward in his chair, he said in a low voice, "Do you not think, Edward, that if I had intended man to fly, I would have given him wings?"

Ed stared blankly back for a second. "I suppose," he ventured.

"You *suppose*? Do you have any idea what this will mean for genetic mixing? All those races I spent so long engineering will be gallivanting off around the globe in your new-fangled flying machines, and soon there'll be nothing but a mish-mash." Henry threw his hands in the air in an exasperated motion. "A mish-mash. And twice as fast, thanks to your little friend out there, little Miss 'Leaves are a lot like people'!"

Ed sat stunned. No promotion, then. Given Henry's mood he thought it best not to say anything. Indeed, Henry seemed to calm down, and let out a long sigh. "Ah, well, it can't be helped now. I need to think what to do with you. Have a day off. Oh, and tell Frank on your way out he needn't bother with the vertical propulsion mechanism we discussed, after all."

△ △ △

Ed spent a nice day off enjoying Katie's new algorithms with Sophie, Demigod of Lorentz Contraction (from whom he'd borrowed the couple of hours). The next day, he was once again called into Henry's office.

Frank was just leaving, looking flustered. “Remember what I said,” Henry called after him, “we could still look at the single-sex thing, even if the three legs won't work.”

Henry absently beckoned Ed in to take a seat, still talking. “I'm more and more convinced that moulding them in our image was a big mistake.” Frank was long gone by this point, and Henry was talking to the air. Ed sat patiently, waiting to be acknowledged, which he finally was, although with the by-now customary surprise.

Henry frowned for a second, then remembered. “Aha! Bumblebees, yes? Oh, and those bloody flying contraptions. Quite a mess you've generated, my boy.”

Ed nodded. “Yes, sir.” No sign of Henry's mood having relented. Yesterday's frolics with Sophie seemed a world away now. Could he really get fired over this? He didn't much fancy being a mortal, especially if Henry's drive to ditch male and female got anywhere. He waited for the verdict, feeling like he was standing in line on the steps of the gallows.

Henry fiddled with his papers before looking up. "I strongly considered letting you go, Edward." Ed winced – he hoped there was a "but" coming. "You simply can't go around taking these sorts of things on your own shoulders. You don't have the experience.

"However, as it happens, a position has opened up in another department that I think will be good for you to take on. It's a demotion to sub-deity level, but I'm sure you understand I didn't have any choice in the matter."

Ed nodded, emotions reeling. Not fired, but demoted. How humiliating. Katie had suffered no such fate. This wasn't fair!

"You'll be working for the Demigod of Natural Forces in the department of Universal Fundamentals. Dave, I think his name is."

Ed wasn't listening by this point. He was trying to fight down his disappointment with internal thoughts of bravado and greatness. He'd show Henry! Whatever this new job was, he was determined to use it as a platform to kick-start his career for real. If Henry couldn't or wouldn't appreciate his talents, then he'd make sure the head of his new department did.

"... your desk by the end of the day," Henry was saying. "And report to Dave in the morning, OK?"

Ed refocussed. "Uh, yes, sir. Thank you." He wasn't sure what he was thanking Henry for, but his boss seemed mollified by his response.

So that was it. A few hours to pack up his things, say goodbye to Katie and Frank and the others, then off to pastures new.

△△△

The Department of Universal Fundamentals was located in the shiny glass-fronted extension to the Woodsville Town Hall, which was perhaps the one upside to all this. The offices were light and airy, unlike the stuffy wood panels and small windows of Henry's domain.

However, Ed's first morning at his new job quickly started to go downhill. First, he was shouted at – no, *bellowed* at by Jean-Claude, Supreme Being of Gravity ("Get out, get out, get out!") who was apparently too busy to see him. Then, when he did get someone to talk to him, it transpired Natural Forces' other office was in the basement. Ed finally found Dave in a room he'd twice ignored, assuming it was a broom cupboard. It was certainly no bigger and smelled faintly of lettuce.

Dave, for his part in the calamity, had no idea who Ed was, and was clearly not expecting him. After a hurried explanation, he finally got the picture. "Oh, I assumed they wouldn't bother replacing Bob. After all, he quit because he had nothing to do."

Ed's heart sank. "Nothing to do? But I thought

he was in charge of all magnetism!"

Dave shrugged. "And what is magnetism used for?"

"Uh, compasses?"

"Yeah. And?"

"Um..."

"Yeah, exactly," Dave said. "That's your desk in the corner. All you have to do is check the planet's magnetic field is in place, so that compasses work properly."

Ed blinked. "That's *it*?"

"Yeah. If you can think of anything else to do with it, knock yourself out."

Ed, feeling worse than ever, sat down at his new desk and slumped down in the chair. He surveyed the abandoned clutter left by his predecessor and tried to muster some of the self-motivation he'd found yesterday in Henry's office. This was even worse than bumblebees!

△ △ △

Dave turned out not to be a bad sort in a morose sort of way. An outlook for which he couldn't be blamed given he was stuck thirty feet underground in a box. He made no effort to act as Ed's boss, preferring to leave him to it, which suited Ed fine.

Not that there was anything to do. It was the dullest, most pointless job ever created. Yet Ed took the bull by the horns, researching his new subject in detail, desperate to find a new angle to make his name.

After three months, and an initial promising success with an invention they were calling 'fridge magnets', Ed found himself struggling. With just magnetism to play with, his hands were tied. The whole concept was too gimmicky to be of much use.

He shared his exasperations with Dave on many occasions, but Dave was too busy keeping atoms held together to care. Though Ed thought he sensed a similar, if more ingrained, look of tedium in his boss's eyes.

Finally, Ed decided to broach the subject directly with Dave. He was understandably wary, given the results of his last foray into something beyond his remit. That time he had material to back it up; this time he had only air.

Ed explained to Dave his desire to do more and make a real impact on the world.

Dave shrugged. “No point. Jean-Claude is so busy holding the universe together he never leaves his office. He doesn't have time to listen to far-fetched ideas from minions like you.”

Ed frowned. He wouldn't be put off so easily. “So, go over his head.”

“To the *Director*? Are you out of your mind? We'd be busted down to mortals before you could say 'Our Father'!”

Ed laughed, realizing Dave could be right, but knowing it didn't bother him anymore. “Come on, Dave, what have you got to lose? Do you really want to be stuck down here for another millennium getting no recognition for all the excellent work you're doing?”

Dave frowned, and Ed thought he might be wavering. He pressed on. “I mean, Jean-Claude sits up there in his shiny new office, while you're stuck down here, and why? You're handling atoms; there are loads more of those to worry about than all the gravitational crap he does upstairs. It should be you up there in that office, not him!”

Dave was silent for a long time, thinking seriously. Ed let him do it while standing expectantly, eyebrows raised.

Eventually, Dave rested his hands in his lap in a resigned gesture and looked up at Ed. “Well,” he said, “now that you mention it, I did have one thought....”

△ △ △

Henry finished reading through Frank's report for the third time, going over in his head exactly how he was going to pitch this to the Director.

He had an audience in an hour. He was convinced this was going to win him big brownie points and the budget he'd always dreamed of.

It had taken a lot of work to get to this point. Mostly Frank's, he freely admitted. The report and the proposal it contained were a long way from the original ideas he'd brought back from the New Project. Nonetheless, they were still, in his own mind at least, impressive and radical. He was sure the Director would feel the same way.

The problem was humanity had not been evolving much – barely at all, in fact – for a long time. They were stagnating. As such, they would never fulfil the immense potential Henry had originally endowed them with. Much as he hated to admit some of his own early design ideas had been flawed, he wasn't afraid to revisit them.

The proposal in front of him would revolutionize the human world. Evolution was back with a vengeance. Specialization was the key.

Extra arms, different scales and proportions, a much more dynamic sexual and gender model. He and Frank had thought of every angle. It would work, and it would be great. Frank had run the numbers, and he was confident the panic level when the first of the 'new' babies were born would be well within tolerance levels.

It was time. Henry grabbed the report (the Director already had a copy, of course) and headed up to the Penthouse Office.

When he arrived and was ushered into the Director's inner sanctum, he was surprised to find himself looking at the backs of several heads gathered around the conference table with the Director at the top. He hadn't been expecting a group session. Moreover, he didn't recognize any of the heads.

"Ah, Henry!" said the Director in his usual jovial manner. "Glad you're here – this concerns you too!"

Henry paused at the foot of the table, unsure what was going on. "Would you like me to give my presentation now, sir?"

The Director smiled. "No need! Read your report – interesting stuff, but I've decided we need to go a different way."

Henry stared. A different way? What different way was there? The proposal was flawless! "But sir..."

The Director continued, failing to recognize Henry's mystified expression. "These clever chaps here have come up with a very exciting idea and an extremely sound roadmap to back it up."

Henry found his louder voice. "Sir, the human race needs to *evolve* – it's clear!"

"I agree. And evolve they will, but not through biology. Through *technology*."

"Technology?" Henry was aghast. Was this a joke?

The Director beamed back at him, oblivious to his discomfort. "Quite. It's an excellent plan. This way, the dominant race gets a sense of achievement in its accomplishments. Rather than some mysterious natural force pushing them on in an unexplained way, they think they're progressing themselves. It'll boost morale."

Henry was getting angry now. "It'll never work!" He'd never trusted technology: a flash in the pan. Biology and evolution was proven methodology.

"I think it will," said the Director, his tone cooler, clearly not liking Henry's reaction. "This proposal sets out the progression of technological evolution for the next several decades. Things called semi-conductors, transistors, integrated circuits, computers, the internet, smart phones. It all sounds jolly exciting to me! Heavens! There's even a plan to allow a human to walk on the moon, imagine that! Why, I see no limit to what can be achieved."

Henry tried to say three things at once, but just ended up letting out an angry, frustrated little splutter.

"Of course, this will require a bit of reorganization," continued the Director. "I'm creating a whole new department to handle this. And that'll leave you to handle the rest of evolution. We only need to worry about the things the humans are actually studying: fruit flies, bumblebees – that sort of thing."

"*Bumblebees*!?" coughed Henry, going red.

"We'll slim down the department and reduce your budget to compensate. Don't worry, Henry, you can sit back and relax a bit."

Henry was disbelieving and desperate by this point. "But you'll need someone to run this new department!"

The Director smiled. "Oh! Of course. How rude of me. I have someone for that already. A terribly creative fellow, responsible for bringing this whole idea together.

"Henry, may I present the new Supreme Being of Technological Development?" He gestured to one of the chairs around the table. Henry turned to look, a sinking feeling of defeat rising from his stomach.

The head in the chair turned slowly around to reveal a smiling face.

"Hello, Henry," said Ed.

# No Substitute

I sighed as I read the sign on the door:

*LenS curry: Is a tot revving Pirate*

I rearranged the letters for the third time in as many days and stepped into my office.

I knew exactly who it was playing with the sign – the kids on the floor below – but I had yet to catch them in the act. Some private investigator I am.

There was only one message on the machine. I prayed it wasn't another little old lady with a lost cat. I seem to have been inundated with a cat exodus of late.

*"Mr. Scurry? My name is David Chambers."*

Well-spoken. Hushed voice: as if he was afraid of being overheard. I get that a lot. People come to a PI when they want something done with a subtlety the police usually can't manage, or with a legality the police usually won't approve of. I take both sorts of cases. Money is money.

*"I, er, have a little matter I'd like you to look into. I wonder if you could give me a call back at work."*

He left his number.

I stared out of the window at the wall opposite for a few moments hoping maybe the world would end, or something more interesting would happen. No luck.

I picked up the phone and dialled the number. He immediately lowered his voice again when he realised who I was, although I suspected he was alone in his office. He wouldn't tell me what it was about over the phone, so we arranged to meet at his house that evening.

I'm not good with mornings, so fortunately, the evening was only a couple of hours away. I spent the intervening time calling animal shelters looking for any newly found cats matching my endless list of newly lost ones.

Around six, I drove out to the address Chambers had given me. It was a way out of town, and as I got further into the area, mentally I began to rub my hands with glee. The houses were getting bigger and bigger as I went on.

Chambers was rolling in it, and that hopefully meant a big payday was on the cards.

I wasn't disappointed. The house was nothing short of a mansion. Several acres of grounds, a huge white façade, endless rooms. I drove up the sweeping gravel driveway and parked my old Tesla next to one of the Porsches.

Chambers opened the door. He was holding a cat

and I half expected him to say: "It's okay. We've found him," and thank me for my time, but fortunately for my bank balance, he didn't. Instead, he shook my hand formally with a grim smile and led me upstairs to his study.

I sat in a big leather armchair, sipping my brandy. Chambers seemed reluctant to say anything, so I set the ball rolling.

"So, Mr. Chambers. What exactly is it I can help you with?"

His awkward frown showed how difficult this was. Saying nothing, he stood up and went to the window and gestured for me to join him.

"My wife," he said simply.

Chambers himself was in good shape, fiftyish, greying at the temples. Probably some high flier in the city. His other half, stretched out in the evening sun by the pool in a one-piece white bathing costume, was the epitome of a trophy wife. She was about half his age, blonde and shapely. And pregnant. Very.

As soon as he'd mentioned his wife, I'd been thinking adultery, but it seemed unlikely she was doing much behind his back in that state except breathing exercises. I wondered if that was her original body, or she'd had an upgrade. The Chambers certainly had the wealth for a VESL and I knew of other husbands who'd favoured that method over more traditional cosmetic surgery to keep their wives looking young. Personally, I disapproved of such things – you only live twice (as the slogan goes), so why use it up before you really need it.

Finally, Chambers spoke up. "Understand, Mr. Scurry, this is very difficult for me. I love my wife and I will not put our marriage at risk. I expect absolute confidentiality from you."

I nodded. "Of course. My clients' wishes always come first. Would you like to tell me exactly what this is about?"

He sighed and sat back down. "My wife, as you can see, is pregnant." Understatement. "The baby should be due any day now." He looked up at me as if asking my permission to go on, so I nodded gently. "My dilemma is this: nine months ago, I was in the middle of a two-month business trip to Korea." Aha! Right after all.

"I see," I said, trying to sound understanding.

"Now, it may be I have my dates wrong, or this has just been a long pregnancy, or a short one. But I'm sure you can understand my suspicion." I nodded. "My wife must not find out about your investigation. If I am wrong, I could not stand her to know I distrusted her."

"I understand, Mr. Chambers."

He went on: "I want you to see if you can track down her movements for the few weeks while I was away and see if there is any indication of foul play that I should know about. Money is no object." I'd wondered when he'd get to that. "Just let me know what you need and you'll have it."

I decided to push my luck. "My fee is five thousand a day... plus expenses. I'll make this case my top priority."

He didn't even bat an eyelid. "Fine."

I barely stopped myself making an audible 'Ker-ching!'.

I stayed a bit longer, probing him for more information that might be useful. I mentioned the possibility of a paternity test, but he was convinced it was impossible to manage that without his wife finding out.

He gave me a list of his staff and told me I could interview them at their homes on their days off, as long as I didn't tell them what the investigation was really about.

△ △ △

So that's exactly what I spent the next week doing, under the pretence of investigating an alleged stalker. A tidy twenty-five grand in the bag and a couple of solid leads to pursue. The biggest problem I hit was that most of the Chambers' staff could barely remember last month, let alone what went on nine months ago. What I did glean was none of them had ever seen any evidence of male visitors while Mr. Chambers was out of the house.

My best lead came from the chauffeur, who kept a precise record of exactly when and where he drove the Chambers. From the copy of those records he had given me, one fact leaped out: Mrs. Chambers didn't go out alone much, but when she did, it was to an exclusive night-club called *El Diablo*.

According to the driver's records, she had been going roughly once every two weeks up until nine months ago. Thereafter, the visits had suddenly stopped.

No more alcohol because of the baby? Or something more sinister?

I also went through Mrs. Chambers' personal spending account – access provided by her husband, without her knowledge – looking for anything suspicious. Sadly, there were so many zeros on the end of all the numbers and so many entries listed as 'Charitable Donation' that it would have been easy to hide any under-the-table transactions. Dead end there.

My most promising lead was *El Diablo*, so the following night I put on my best going-out rags and went to check the place out.

It was in the expensive end of town. Those on the guest list waltzed in with a nod to the bouncer. Everyone else, including me, had to line up. It took over an hour to get in, but we were entertained while we waited: a juggler and a magician moved up and down the line, showing off impromptu acts of skill and sleight of hand.

Also showing his wares to the line was a guy selling Shims – just the novelty stick-on type that projected images like coloured skin-designs, enhanced cleavage and a dozen other cosmetic boosts. I could see several people down the line who had made use of his services, and a few more elaborate examples which probably required actual implants. I turned his offer down: twice the price of an official Shimmer outlet. Besides, the way I look is the main thing that lets me fly under the radar in these situations. It's also why I became a PI in the first place.

When I was eight years old I was killed by a hit-and-run driver while out playing on my bike. Back in those days, CANs were brand new – not like now where every ambulance has a shelf full of them. But, I got lucky: the paramedics responding to the emergency call were part of a trial roll-out of the technology and they took the life-saving decision to decant me before my brain activity faded.

Fortunately, that same trial meant my parents were able to get a new body for me at a massive discount. It was just as well. We weren't well-off. It would have taken them the rest of their lives and their whole retirement fund to save up at normal prices. All the while with me sat on the shelf in my Cognitive Access Node oblivious to the passage of time. *You only live twice* indeed. They should add: *if you're filthy rich.*

Custom-grown VESLs didn't exist back then. There was no near-duplicate synthetic version of yourself to wake up in and go on with your life as if nothing had happened. My parents were given a choice of ten new bodies for me; the same ten faces everyone had to pick from. They chose number three.

I was angry at first. Staring at a different face in the mirror each morning. It wasn't me. It took some getting used to. I wanted justice, or maybe revenge, on the guy who hit me.

So, when the police officers showed up at our door to let us know they'd caught the guy and he was going to prison for a long time, they became my heroes. From then on, I wanted to be a cop.

Except of course it's only recently they've started letting anyone but Original Humans serve on the force. So, with that dream killed along with my first body, I did the next best thing and set up shop for myself.

Since I was eight I've had this face. Number three. There are over a hundred thousand people with this face on the planet now. I could be any one of them. I blend in. I'm anonymous. That suits me just fine.

I finally got into the club. I thought I'd misheard the cashier when she told me how much the entrance fee was, but I reminded myself it was all on expenses and paid up.

The club itself was classy with a sort of subtropical theme. All the waitresses had red skin, horns and a forked tail to go with the *El Diablo* name.

I found a quiet corner, ordered a cocktail, reminded myself I was here to work, and scanned the room for anything that might have a bearing on the case.

Pretty much everyone in the room was young, rich and beautiful. I felt out of place.

There was plenty of action to be had too, and everyone seemed to be looking for it. I'd seen hardly anyone come in as a couple, but plenty had paired up inside and were being none too discreet about it. I even had a couple of young ladies come up to my table and ask if I'd like to dance. I was flattered, and the pale-green elf-girl almost broke my resolve, but I never mix business and pleasure.

Over the course of the next couple of hours, I watched the clientèle and the staff: mapping their behaviour, looking for anything suspicious. There was one guy in particular who caught my attention. His look fit the club, and I guessed he was part of the whole package. He had small horns protruding from his forehead, and I couldn't see any sign of it being a Shim, so I guessed it was either make-up or expensive implants – you can spot the cheap stick-ons even in dim lighting like the club if you know what to look for.

He spent the evening wandering from table to table, mostly those occupied by attractive young women. He ended up at table alone with a stunning redhead who was poured into the tiniest little blue dress that (naturally) matched her eyes.

I asked my demon-waitress who he was when she next came to fill up my cocktail from her giant pitcher.

"Oh, that's Mr. Cortez. He's the club owner." She smiled revealing pointed fangs – nice touch – and moved on to the next table of thirsty patrons.

Cortez – El Diablo, himself? – seemed to have a natural charisma and magnetism. Everyone liked him, everyone was happy when he talked to them.

And the young lady at his table seemed all too happy to follow him into a private area of the club. Excellent tactic: open your own club; ensure only attractive available women attend; take your pick. I suspected he had a different one accompany him into the back room each night. They might even have considered it an honour.

With Cortez gone, I turned my attention back to the rest of the room, but found little of interest. I was beginning to think this lead was turning into a dead end. There was nothing in the club to suggest anything underhanded was going on. Cortez seemed to be the perfect host: genial and charming.

I was about to give up the whole thing and go home to bed when the redhead from earlier reappeared from the same doorway she had disappeared into with Cortez. I was surprised: I'd expected it to be an all-night session. Perhaps Cortez hadn't played his cards right, after all.

The girl looked a little unsure of herself, stumbling in her impressive heels a couple of times. She also kept reaching up and massaging the back of her neck.

As she passed me, she pulled her hand away from her neck, wincing and looked down at a few spots of blood smeared across her palm. Maybe there was something here after all. What exactly had Cortez been up to in the back room?

It was a tenuous lead at best. Most likely Cortez had tried to inject her with something – a drug to increase libido maybe – and it'd gone wrong and spooked the girl. On the other hand, it was the only lead I had, bar following up on a few unpromising half-remembered comments from the Chambers' other staff. I decided Cortez was worth further investigation.

I got up from my table and went to sit at the end of the bar nearest the door into the back room. The door was a faked-up wooden affair with no windows. No clue as to what lay behind it.

I waited an hour. After no one came in or out, I decided to give up and see if I could see anything from the outside.

It was late by that point, and I was surprised to

see there was still a smallish line waiting to get in. The street entertainers were no more though: no need to pull in the punters when the club was already full.

I circled the entire building from the outside, trying to work out how the interior walls mapped to the shape of the building outside. The entire back of the building was walled off with no windows. I cursed under my breath.

The only way I was going to get into that area of the building was through that door.

By that point I was dog tired, so decided it was time to call it a night and head home for some well-earned sleep.

△△△

The sleep did me a world of good and I awoke refreshed and ready to face the world – with no more leads than I'd had the night before.

I called Chambers and let him know how the investigation was going, explaining I only had one shaky lead and asking if he wanted me to pursue it. To my relief he said yes, anything I could find out would be useful. Continuing the case meant continuing the flow of money in the right direction, so I was happy.

My objective was to get into the back room of *El Diablo* and find out exactly what Cortez was up to. I could think of two ways of doing that.

I could break in, which would only help if there was a place to hide so I could watch Cortez at work in the evening. Assuming I could get past the bouncers and security cameras. Or, alternatively, I could get Cortez to take me back there and show me himself.

I didn't like the implications of option two, but it seemed much more likely to succeed than option one. The only way Cortez was going to show me what he was doing back there was if he was trying to do it to me, which meant a rather elaborate disguise of a type I wasn't keen on using.

People use Shims to change their appearance all the time, be it for pleasure, fun or business. The stick-ons are fun, but low fidelity – you can easily spot they're holographic projections from the right angle. The implant type is much more realistic. Other than in bright sunlight you'd need to stick your finger through the image to be able to tell – but they're limited in size, and require minor surgery to install.

Neither of those was going to achieve what I needed. That meant if I wanted to set myself up with a convincing disguise, I was going to have to go outside the usual (read: legal) channels. That's where Harry came in.

I don't know Harry and he doesn't know me, and that's the way we like to keep it. Harry is a man who knows how to get things done. How and where he gets his information and contacts I don't know, but I know for a fact he's not strictly on the level. Despite that, Harry is one of the good guys, and I've never had any problem with his services. He always delivers, and he makes sure you know he will – by charging through the nose.

I picked up the phone and dialled. “Harry? It's Len. Need a favour.”

“I'm listening.”

I described what I needed and waited for him to stop laughing. “Man, I'd love to see this.”

“Yeah, yeah, ha, bloody ha. Can you find someone to do it?”

He didn't hesitate. “Yeah. I'll call you back in an hour.”

I spent the time looking for lost cats. Honest.

Exactly an hour later, Harry phoned back. He gave me a time and a place.

The place was up near the university campus, as I suspected it would be. I'd done this sort of thing a couple of times before. The ingestible nano-Shims that can manage full-body images by placing tiny projectors under the entire surface of your skin are illegal for anything except government use and ongoing R&D. The best way to get hold of them was to tempt a college student from the science lab with extra beer funds. They'd be in trouble if caught, but the lure of beer is a beautiful thing.

It was still a shady affair. Three o'clock in the morning; deserted courtyard. I stood freezing half to death wrapped in a thick overcoat, hood up, in the shadows of one corner. At a few minutes past the hour, I saw him emerge into the dull light of the opposite corner of the courtyard and head towards me. He too was wrapped up beyond recognition.

He held out a gloved hand proffering a small vial of clear liquid. "Here. Drink it now. I don't want you selling it on to anyone else."

A fair enough position. I opened the vial and swallowed it down. It didn't taste of anything except water and for a moment I wondered if I was being ripped off. Then someone set fire to my skin. At least, that's how it felt. I doubled over and let out a muffled cry. The pain only lasted a couple of seconds and when I regained my senses, he was already gone.

I decided to wait until I got home to see what the damage was. There was no complaints line for this sort of endeavour, so I'd have to make do with whatever I had, regardless.

As soon as I got home, I headed up to the full-length mirror in the bathroom and flung off the overcoat, under which I was wearing precisely nothing.

Last time I'd used a disguise like this it'd been significantly less radical. I thought I'd had plenty of practice getting used to a different face in the mirror, but the dark-haired beauty in the revealing red dress staring back at me now was so utterly unfamiliar I almost turned to look behind me to see where she was. It was pretty much what I'd asked for, but that didn't stop it from freaking me out a bit. The student had got somewhat carried away. The projected me was drop-dead gorgeous with curves that threatened to evade the constraints of the dress at any moment – impossible, of course, given both were just part of the same hologram.

Still, I knew one thing for certain: Cortez would be at my table in a second.

I went back downstairs to pick up the parcel from Harry that I knew would be there. Untraceable, of course. It contained fake ID, a purse and joke-shop gel which increases the pitch of your voice when you swallow it, all to complete the disguise. Like I said, Harry is good to work with.

It was four in the morning. I pulled on a t-shirt and pyjama bottoms which vanished my non-existent curves as the projectors were blocked. I couldn't do anything about my head, so I avoided mirrors while I got ready for bed.

△△△

The next morning, I didn't want to risk blowing my disguise by going into work, so I worked from home: going through the entries in Mrs. Chambers' bank account transactions and making a few calls to verify all the charities referenced really did exist. All but two checked out straight away. The others presented possible leads, but nothing solid without more investigation and I didn't have time to look into them further: it was time to get ready to revisit *El Diablo*.

I grabbed a shower which turned out to be easiest with my eyes closed. Trying to get washed when it looks like you're fully-dressed and female is best done by feel.

Once I'd dried off I grabbed the accessories Harry had provided and checked out my final appearance. I'd wanted to give the impression of being a bored trophy wife with a rich husband: the same role as Mrs. Chambers. The look worked.

I couldn't wear a coat without spoiling the effect. While I was the only one who would know it, I didn't fancy walking through town stark naked, freezing off bits of anatomy you couldn't even tell I possessed. So, I ordered a cab to take me to the club.

As I suspected, the bouncer on the door of *El Diablo* let me straight in after he had wiped his chin off the floor. There were a few catcalls from the men in the line along with a couple of less appreciative comments from the women. If only they'd known the truth.

My table from the night before was free, but I avoided sitting at it. Realistically, as long as I didn't move around too much and the lighting remained this dim, my disguise was so complete there was no chance anyone would make any correlation between the sexy young thing I resembled and the nondescript guy in his mid-thirties from the night before. But, it often helps to be a little paranoid in my trade.

I placed myself about two-thirds of the way down the bar, towards the end nearest the door into the back, but not too close. All the barmen were wonderfully helpful in their competition to look down the front of my non-existent dress.

I kept it simple and ordered a scotch.

Cortez didn't show for a couple of hours and I was beginning to worry it was his night off. I did see a few faces I recognised from the night before in the interim, including the cute green elf-girl, who was now sporting a bluer shade of skin, but still had the pointed ears. I almost nodded to her in acknowledgement, before I caught myself – she had no way to recognise me from the night before.

"Another drink for the lady!" Cortez had slid into the seat next to me without me even noticing. The barman replenished my beverage instantly and then left us alone. Cortez turned to face me, "Alberto Cortez. Charmed. And you are?"

"Lisa," I said, using the name on the fake ID from Harry.

He was smooth and charming, which was fine by me. It made it easy to spin out my back-story for him and set myself up as the perfect rich, bored housewife. He threw in a few questions intended to establish whether anyone would miss me if I ended up staying later at the club.

My plan went off the rails when we moved to sit at a private table and he asked another of the more attractive patrons to join us – a pretty Asian girl, named Ji, who didn't say much. Things got back on track when he invited us both back into his private area for some 'fun'.

I'd achieved my goal. I hoped I was going to discover more than a horny club owner looking for a romp with a couple of pretty girls.

For the first time since I set out on my crazy subterfuge, I began to feel a little nervous. Perhaps I should have staked the place out for a few more nights. The redhead from the night before could have been a one-off. Maybe he was only looking for sex. Mrs. Chambers' state backed up that thought. He was in for a nasty surprise if he tried it on with me!

I tried to push my doubts from my mind as he took us through that elusive doorway. I had a gut instinct something more sinister was on the cards, and my instincts usually serve me well.

The back room was nothing special – a small, well-stocked bar, soft leather armchairs, a rather tasteless life-size gold statue of a scantily-clad young lady and a couple of closed doors leading off into other rooms. At least one of which, I presumed, was a bedroom.

He was all smiles. "Have a seat, ladies. Can I get you a drink?" He gestured at the selection behind the bar. "It's all the best stuff. I pride myself on insisting only on the top-shelf."

I asked for a scotch and settled into one of the armchairs. Ji ordered a Martini and did likewise.

I didn't see what he did, but, as soon as both of us were firmly in our seats, wrist restraints snapped into place from the arms, locking us into the chairs.

"Hey! What's the big idea?" complained Ji. I said nothing. This was, after all, what I'd come to see. I subtly tested the restraints. I was a lot stronger than I looked to him and I was fairly sure I could overpower him if needed, but not if I was bound to the chair. While they seemed solid, there was a little bit of give. I didn't dare pull harder until I knew what was going on.

Cortez's demeanour changed completely. He emerged from behind the bar, drinks discarded. The smile was gone, replaced by a hard expression.

"Sorry ladies, I hope you won't take this personally. There'll be no hanky-panky this evening, but I do have a couple of business transactions to run through. And you're both in a perfect position to help me out."

He opened one of the other doors from the room, and a scruffy youth wandered out. He looked to be in his early twenties and rather flustered.

Cortez became his genial self again, although there were serious undertones this time. "My dear fellow," he addressed the boy. "You get first pick. Which will it be?"

For a moment, I thought Cortez was trying to sell us off as prostitutes or worse, but when the boy spoke, the whole frightening picture began to fall into place.

He looked at me with a look between lust and horror and finally pointed to Ji. "Her. If I've got to be a chick, there's no way I want tits that big."

Cortez smirked; he was enjoying this. "Very well." He went behind the bar and retrieved a CAN and before I could do anything he pressed it against the base of Ji's skull.

She was frantic by this point. "What the hell are you doing, Cortez? Do you know who my husband is? I'll have the cops down on you quicker than you can think if you don't let me go this second!"

I pulled harder at the metal bracelets around my wrists. They moved a bit more, but still held. Cortez just smiled that unnerving smile. "I think not." He grabbed Ji's hair to steady her head and switched on the CAN and I watched in horror as she convulsed and went silent as the device's tendrils invaded her brain and sucked it clean of memories, personality and knowledge. Even if I could break the restraints, it was too late now for Ji. Her body would die in a couple of minutes. What exactly was Cortez trying to achieve here?

He stashed the CAN containing Ji's mind and pulled out another, but this one was unlike anything I'd seen before – heavily modified for some unknown purpose. He used it to decant the boy's mind, leaving his slumped body on the floor where it fell. Then he took the CAN over to Ji's barely-alive body and pressed it to the back of her neck.

What the hell was he doing? You can't implant a mind into a human body. You need a VESL for that – they're grown with brains with completely different wiring to allow for the upload; hence why they're only "virtually equivalent" synthetic lifeforms. I'd also read the decanting process does serious damage to the human brain – there's no way you'd want to live in one afterwards even if it was possible. You'd be at risk from all sorts of neurological conditions and psychoses.

Nonetheless, it seemed the impossible was exactly what Cortez was planning. The CAN was reactivated. Ji's body convulsed again as tendrils re-entered her brain. It took a couple of minutes before the CAN indicated upload was complete and he pulled the device free. The tendrils left small trails of blood from the holes they'd bored. A moment later Ji's body became animated again. First a gasp, and then, "Fucking hell!" as she looked down at herself. Cortez had got hold of technology that could put a decanted mind back into an ordinary human body!

I wondered if there was any of Ji left over in there? Might he have access to her memories? Her personality? VESLs were always blank slates before upload. Who knew who the person Cortez had just created really was? Maybe that would make it easier for the kid to pass himself off as Ji without being too suspicious.

Cortez released the restraints on the chair and pulled the former boy to her feet. "Take her purse and walk out through the club. I never want to see you again after that. Understood?"

Still looking shell-shocked at being a petite Asian woman, she nodded, and stumbled from the room in unfamiliar heels, rubbing her neck. I wondered what sort of trouble the boy had been in to drive him to these lengths – stealing someone's life – and who was bank-rolling his escape route.

Cortez was in big business. It looked to me like he was pulling off a number of these 'transactions' a week, at a tidy profit. How could he possibly be getting away with it without anyone noticing? I supposed no one was going missing except the ones stealing the lives of the girls, and they were unlikely to be missed.

The case of the Chambers fell into place. Mrs. Chambers was not the same person she'd been nine months ago. She was an interloper, uploaded into a stolen body by Cortez for a sizeable fee. But she'd made a mistake. Too keen to try out the new body in her inherited husband's absence, she'd got herself pregnant – maybe even by Cortez himself, although he gave the impression of not being that sloppy. The real Mrs. Chambers was sadly lost forever. I doubted Cortez kept his stolen minds. Why buy more CANs when you can overwrite them?

I was next. I had two things in my favour: the element of surprise, and the fact I wasn't an Original Human. A CAN wouldn't work on me; I'd had my second chance at life already. You can't decant a VESL – something Cortez was about to find out. Nonetheless, I was starting to worry what he might do to cover his tracks when he found out he couldn't affect me. The sheer criminality and scale of what he was up to meant it would be easy to bring him down, but only if I escaped with my life. I sensed the restraint on my right was about to give, but I didn't have long.

Cortez brought out his next client. An old woman, maybe in her nineties, looking reasonably well to do. Her reasons for this business deal were pretty obvious – Cortez's rates, while no doubt steep, were presumably more palatable than buying a VESL. With only around twenty years left on her clock and those spent in decline it was time for an upgrade.

She looked me up and down as if I was a piece of meat and a cruel smile slowly formed on her weathered features. "Yes, this will do nicely. Excellent work, Alberto."

"Thank you, ma'am. I do my best." Cortez was laying the smarm on with a trowel now. One of his better paying clients.

Next came the moment of truth. Cortez came over to me with the CAN – I'd been right, he intended to overwrite Ji's previous recording – and I struggled much less subtly against my bonds; the situation was getting dangerous. One of two things was about to happen if I couldn't break free. The attempt to decant me would miraculously work, in which case I was in serious trouble, or Cortez would realise his plan wasn't going to work as smoothly as he might like. What he'd do then, I had no idea.

I felt his hand grip the top of my head and waited for something to happen. Beads of sweat began forming on my brow – that would quickly flush out the nano-Shims if I wasn't careful. Maybe that wouldn't be a bad outcome by this point.

"Shit!" Nothing happened. I was extremely relieved, although my life was still in danger.

"You bitch! I checked your neck – there are no marks!" There were, but the give-away leftovers of the upload process were covered by the Shim. Clearly he knew to only target real humans, and had thought he'd checked. He was furious and a little off-kilter, not sure what to do to rectify the situation.

My worst fear was he would choose to kill me and

dispose of the body, so I took a big risk to try and defuse the situation.

"It's over, Cortez. You're under arrest. The place is swarming with police. There's nowhere to run." It was a huge bluff, of course, but I was hoping he'd panic and try to save his own skin first and foremost. Free and on the run was better than locked in a cell.

His eyes were wild now, trying to guess if I was being truthful. It was enough to distract him for the moment I needed to pull my arm free of the wristband. The action sent my arm flying upwards towards his head, and so I let it keep going until my fist connected awkwardly with his chin. He staggered backwards, startled. It was only a glancing blow, but it gave me enough time to pull at the other arm. Using both hands I easily broke the restraint. I was free from the chair. I stood up and turned around to face him.

His initial shock had turned to anger, and he was advancing on me. I still had an advantage – he thought I was a weak woman he could easily overpower. In fact, he was so overconfident he didn't even go for a punch – he reached around my head and tried to grab my hair. The thick hair that was a hologram. His hand passed right through it, and his momentum carried him forwards, off-balance. It was easy to grab his shoulders, rotate my body out of the way and give him a good push to help him on his way to falling to the ground.

He got as far as "What the hell..." before I followed up with a solid punch to the nose, which put him out cold. Alberto Cortez was down.

The old woman was gone – she'd understood trouble when she'd seen it and cut her losses.

With difficulty, I dragged Cortez into the chair with the still-functioning restraints and found the button behind the bar to reactivate them. It wouldn't hold him indefinitely but would do for now.

Next, I poured myself a large scotch and gargled with it to dislodge the voice-changing gel from my throat before swallowing down a couple more fingers of the amber liquid. I don't much care for violence and I needed to steady myself against the after-effects of the adrenaline rush the brief fight with Cortez had generated. The mirror behind the bar revealed I'd sweated so much the nano-Shims had been completely flushed out of my skin in many places.

I needed to call the police, but the current situation was not conducive to the smoothest route to Cortez's arrest. In a room with a dead body and an unconscious, bloody-nosed, restrained and nominally respected local business man, I was the half-naked one using the illegal disguise. It wasn't a conversation I wanted to have.

Instead I looked behind the second door in the back of the room and was relieved to find I was right – it was indeed a bedroom. Better still, Cortez had a wardrobe with spare clothing in it. I pulled on a shirt, some slacks and a pair of loafers, which fit well enough, and returned to check on him – still out cold.

With the two CANs under my arm as vital evidence, I then headed out through the other door in the back of the room – the one from which the kid and old lady had emerged. It opened to reveal stairs leading downwards and it turned out to pass under the alleyway behind the club and let out of a door on the other side, which is why I'd missed that entrance when scoping the place out the previous night.

Only once free of *El Diablo* and a couple of streets away did I pull my phone from the purse and make the call. I gave only the outline of a plausible story to start with, emphasising the urgency of getting someone over to the club to arrest him before he woke up and escaped his restraints. I told them I had key physical evidence and that I'd deliver it in person shortly.

First though, I needed to get into proper clothes and flush the rest of the Shims from my system. I hailed a cab, went home, took a hot bath and got changed, before heading back out to give the CANs to the police.

The story I spun was based heavily on what had happened, but I glossed over the fact the second girl in the room was actually me. Instead I suggested I'd been suspicious of Cortez and had found my way in, having discovered the back entrance to the club. I'd listened to his devious acts, overpowered him when the opportunity arose and then fled the club to keep the evidence safe from any of his lackeys that might have arrived on the scene.

Clearly the police believed there'd been foul play of some sort, but my story was a little far-fetched, so I was under a bit of suspicion for a couple of weeks. They looked for the other witness: the curvy brunette in the red dress. Obviously without much success. Fortunately, once they uploaded Ji into a new VESL and she confirmed the parts of the story she was conscious for, it got a lot easier. I went from suspect to hero.

Of course, there weren't happy endings all round. The woman posing as Mrs. Chambers was arrested. David was understandably devastated when he found out the truth.

Who knows how many others have had their lives destroyed by Cortez and how many people are living with interlopers treating them as loved ones, completely unaware.

Cortez named a few names in his interrogation, but I doubt we'll ever know for sure the extent of his operation. I never heard any more about the bootleg CAN that can upload to a human brain, but I'll bet it's being researched with great interest in a lab somewhere.

Everyone involved that night will serve time.

They tracked down the old lady quickly enough although she got off lightly given her age and limited involvement. The ex-boy, who, it turned out, had an outstanding murder charge on top of everything else, will not be seen for a long time. Although I heard there might be an element of relief – the life of a trophy wife perhaps not having been the escape that was hoped for.

Cortez himself was given the harshest punishment available: decanted; his body destroyed; his CAN put into long-term storage. He'll get a parole review every hundred years, but it's hard to make your case when you're just a block of data on a crystal in a warehouse. He deserved as much. More maybe. He'd murdered who knows how many people and abused what should be beneficial technology for personal financial gain. I hope they store his CAN in the appropriate location – after all, he prides himself on being top-shelf....

△ △ △

*enc SLurry: Invigorate Pert vista*

"Damn those kids!"

# Devastation

## *Watchers II*

Have you ever loved? Did you cling to every heartbeat as it echoed through your soul? I have. Once. But I was too late.

If you stand on the cliffs, overlooking the bridge, early in the morning when the mist covers the bay, it's almost as if the rest of the world ceases to exist. You slip into a silent, lonely existence of your own. I find it tranquil. The image of the grand suspension bridge fading eerily into the fog, points the way back to civilisation.

I used to come out on a Sunday morning when I needed some time to myself, to think, or maybe to dream. It's amazing the directions a mind can take if it's left to wander.

The arrival of the Watchers brought a whole new dimension to that, of course. The addition to the panorama of a huge spaceship, floating impossibly over the water, rather captured the imagination. At first, I thought they'd ruined my favourite view. As time passed and their benevolent nature became apparent, I came to like the idea of them watching over us and the updated scenery became reassuring.

That morning, I first saw her appear phantom-like from the silvery mist blanketing the hilltop. An angel descending the clouds from heaven. It seemed like that to me, anyway. She was a vision; I found myself staring, unblinking as she glided down to the railing to gaze out over the cliffs.

At first, I didn't think she'd seen me standing there. It's sometimes hard to see your own feet up there when the fog is thick. When she spoke, it was like a warm breeze brushing past my ears. I don't know if she was speaking to me, or just out to the bay, but it didn't matter.

In those short few seconds, my heart was already lost.

"You can almost see your soul out here." It was a peculiar way to start a conversation. Oddly, I thought I knew what she meant. Sometimes, with nothing else to distract, the only place you can look is inwards. I wasn't sure what to say, or even whether I should say anything at all.

"Don't you think?" Still she didn't look at me, remaining immersed in the seeming nothingness of the mist.

"Y-yes," I stammered.

"Almost. But not quite. You can never quite see

deep enough. Believe me, I've tried."

I wondered if she was referring to the ship. The Watchers' strange obsession with resurrecting long-dead figures from history had led some to speculate they were collecting souls. Storing them in those huge ships in case they wanted to bring anyone back in future. Religious communities were divided over the issue. On the one hand proof of the existence of souls would be a confirmation of their beliefs. On the other, if the Watchers were preventing them reaching heaven, that was a problem.

"Maybe one day they'll share their secrets on that front," I said, nodding towards the ship. I hoped I was on the right wavelength.

She turned to me. Those eyes. Big and so very sad. Looking into mine, staring into the core of my being.

"One day," she said, simply, before returning to her communion with the bay.

I moved a little closer. "So, do you..."

"Come here often?" For a moment I thought I detected the merest hint of a laugh pass her lips, but instantly it was gone. "Sometimes. When I get lonely."

A strange thing to say. In all my tens of dawn visits, she was the first person I had ever encountered.

"But isn't it more lonely up here?"

"You're here, aren't you?"

She had a point. “Normally, though, it's deserted.”

“Yes. I suppose.”

I decided I'd better try and steer the conversation back to something more mundane, before I lost my way completely.

“You're from the city?”

“I was.” She brought new meaning to the term monosyllabic. Yet I got the impression she had so much more to say, bottled up inside, trapped by whatever tragedy could drive such a creature to this much sadness.

“Oh, you moved away?”

“You could say that.” She turned to me once more and the sun chose that moment to break through the clouds. It illuminated her from behind and gave her a golden aura, making the whole scene somewhat unreal. “I have to go now.” She smiled. My heart skipped a beat.

“Wait. I don't even know your name...” She had already turned and begun walking back into the haze.

“You will,” she called back gently. I wanted to run after her, but somehow my feet seemed rooted to the spot. My heart thumped in my chest.

The rest of the day dragged on forever. It sounds weird, but I ached for her. She had captured my heart completely in those few moments. I knew I would return to the cliff top every morning until I knew her name.

As it was, I only had to wait until the next morning, but I didn't hear it from her sweet lips, rather from the front page of the news.

*Woman's Body Found.* I recognised her face immediately. She had jumped from the cliffs. My heart felt as if it had taken the same journey. Such a short time. Too short. She had been taken from me.

I read the rest of the story, tears in my eyes, condemning myself. I could have, should have, stopped her. I could see she was upset over something. Why did I do nothing?

△ △ △

I know now I could not have saved her. The police said her body had been lying, undiscovered, for nearly a week.

I still don't know what happened on that Sunday morning. Perhaps the Watchers really do collect souls and I somehow encountered hers in transit. All I know is, wherever she is now, she has my heart with her.

This morning, the fog is light. The bridge looks magnificent and the sun glints off the Watchers' ship. Is she somehow up there? I've come here every week in the hope I might encounter her again, with no luck. The loss of what could have been is hard to accept. I need to move on.

I take in the view one final time. The railing at my back, the spectacular vista spreads out before me. I look up at the ship as I step forward into the abyss. I pray they will let me be with her again.

Have you ever loved? Did you cling to every lingering, aching heartbeat as it echoed through the empty, bottomless chasm of your soul?

# Parallels

## *First*

"What's your name, kid?"

I fight to get the word out — throat constricted, heart thumping — "Aaron." I can't believe I'm sitting here in the presence of Jack Turner. *The* Jack Turner, best grifter ever to play the field.

He walks behind my chair, smoke drifting behind him, across my face before the whining ceiling fan pushes it away. I fight the urge to turn, trying to stay calm. I'm terrified if I lose sight of him, it'll all dissolve into a dream.

"Done many jobs before?" asks Jack, sliding back into view, eyeing me critically.

My heart misses a beat. Is it a trick question? What does he want to hear? Does he want a fresh, unknown face, or a seasoned pro? I opt for honesty, "One or two. Small time stuff."

He nods slowly, inhaling his own second-hand smoke as if to clear the haze in the small room. "Five of us on the job. Your cut's ten percent. OK?"

I nod, not daring to breathe in case he changes his mind. I'm in.

He slides a crumpled page from yesterday's paper across the table. On it is scribbled a name and address in thick black marker. "That's the mark. I want you on the inside within the week. Now, beat it."

I grin, "Thanks, Mister Turner," but he's already out the door. I stand, feeling tall, and head out to find Abigail Skipham of 15 Murraygate.

## Second

"What's your name, kid?"

"Aaron, sir." I pull at the base of my jacket, as I stand, waiting, awkward, trying to look respectable.

"You're not at school, son. Call me Mister Turner. Now, you make sure you have my niece back by eleven, you understand?"

"Yes, Mister Turner." He seems nice enough in a stern sort of way. I will Abigail to appear, wanting to get away.

"What're you kids planning on... ah, here's Abigail. You all ready, honey?"

Abigail is a vision as she sweeps into the hallway, wearing slightly less than her uncle might approve of. Although if this is the case, he shows no sign.

She kisses him on the cheek and grabs my arm all in one swift motion, "Seeya later, Uncle Jack!"

Before I have a chance to say my own good-bye and maybe salvage a good impression, we're already down the driveway and stepping out onto Murraygate.

## Third

"What's your name, kid?"

I fight to get the word out, fists clenched, knuckles white. Arsehole. "Aaron."

Detective Inspector Jack Turner doesn't like me, and it's mutual. He can see my rage, barely held in check by the handcuffs and the burly constable in the corner. "Now, why don't you calm down and tell us why you killed her?"

I want to yell. It comes out a hiss. "For the fifth time. I did not kill Abigail."

He nods, frowning. Then, he's in my face, leaning across the desk, nose to nose. "Then could you please explain why we have an eye witness who swears they watched you come out of the alley where we found her body, covered in blood?"

"It's your job to explain that. Not mine." I feel clever for a moment until he pulls the chair from under me. It hurts — I'm still handcuffed to it.

"Do not mess around with me, kid. If you really didn't do it, then you need to get a lot more helpful, fast, or you're going to prison for a very long time." He stares me out until he sees me relent. The floor is cold, after all. I gingerly take his proffered hand and lever myself back into the chair.

"Okay. I'll tell you what I know. It all started on Murraygate."

## First

Murraygate runs down the edge of the Gull Cliffs. All the big houses with their panoramic views are in stark contrast to the dingy streets below. Directly under the Skipham residence is an old alleyway with a load of abandoned warehouses. It's from there I first observe Abigail, looking for my in.

Now I have it, as I watch the ambulance, the broken ladder and the concerned faces. It's time to set myself up in the window cleaning trade.

It only takes me an hour to buy the stuff, but I wait until the next day before approaching the house, not wanting to be *too* convenient.

The man of the house, Abigail's uncle, is all too keen to sign me on. He tells me the sad tale of his own window cleaner. We laugh about the irony of my timing.

The windows gleam in the sun and I'm well paid. It's not hard to extend my repertoire. Gardening, car washing, general maintenance. Soon I'm a permanent fixture.

Abigail comes and goes. She's pretty. Sometimes I watch her through the windows. Part of me thinks it's a shame we're going to deprive her of her trust fund. Mostly I can't wait for Jack and the others to start the job.

## Second

We skip down Murraygate, hand in hand, following the edge of the Gull Cliffs. We bypass all the big houses; ignore the panoramic views. We descend into the city below. Abigail knows a spot in the alley right below her house. It's there I get my first kiss.

Abigail wants more. At first, I'm a little shocked. This is not how I'd imagined it. Weeks to pluck up the courage to ask her out. Now, on our first date, she's unbuttoning her blouse and pressing my hand to her chest.

I look her in the eyes. She smiles invitingly; pretty. Part of me worries I'm depriving her of her innocence. Mostly I'm enthusiastic about the job.

## Third

"Murrygate runs down the side of the Gull Cliffs. Big houses looking out over the shittiest end of town. Kings of the castle, you know the place?"

The DI nods, sitting, relaxed now he's got me to talk. "Go on."

"So, I'm walking down the road, minding my own business, when I see this girl come out of one of the big houses. Short skirt, nice legs. She's with some guy, out on a date, I guess. I don't pay them much more attention."

"And this was Abigail?"

"Yeah. So, they get a bit further on, heading down into the old part of town, and the guy seems to be getting a bit frisky. Hands wandering, if you know what I mean. He leads her into this alley."

"And you reckon she's not so keen to go?" asks the inspector.

"Exactly. And being the good Samaritan I am, I decide to check it out. Only, as I pass the house — the one she came out of — there's this other guy. Turns out he's the gardener or window cleaner or whatever, right?"

"Mind if I smoke?" He's already lit up.

"Knock yourself out. So, this guy's seen the whole thing too, and he's pissed about it, so we decide to go down and check it out. See if the girl's OK."

He nods, "And so, you go into the alley?"

"Bingo. We sneak in trying to stay out of sight at first. It's pretty dark by this point, so we don't see them until we're on top of them. He's just standing over her, knife in his hand. Blood everywhere; he's stabbed her. I panic and rush forward to try to revive her. Part of me worries he'll attack me too, but he doesn't move, so I get on with the job."

## Convergence

The DI nods, getting up again and walking behind my chair, spreading thick smoke across the room. The whining fan blows it into my face.

For a moment, the room seems to blur. It's like I'm watching three different detectives walk back into view. I blink the smoke from my eyes, and things get better. My head is splitting though. It's hard to concentrate. I try to focus on the inspector as he sits down and leans across the table. What was his name again?

"Aaron, *you're* the handyman at the Skipham residence."

My brain won't work. I try to make sense of his words. Oddly, confusingly, I remember it. Getting the job, the window cleaner with the broken ladder, and the broken leg. I remember staring at Abigail through the windows, thinking she was pretty. It took me weeks to pluck up the courage to ask her out.

"*You* took Abigail out on a date tonight. We checked with her uncle," he confirms.

It's still hard to think. "Right...." The uncle; nice but stern. I made a bad impression. What was his name?

He leans in close again, words coming slowly,

softly, "You killed Abigail Skipham."

I frown at him, not feeling myself. "Why the hell would I do that?"

"To cover up the fact you'd cleaned out her trust fund safe."

I nod; the room seems hazy. "Trust fund," I echo. Saying the words makes it clearer. Suddenly I remember the job. She'd said yes to the date, but it wasn't real. As soon as we were alone, she unbuttoned her blouse and pressed my hand to her chest – over her locket. The locket no longer containing the key to the safe. She knew. I panicked. The knife....

I'd blown the job. I'd let down the greatest grifter ever to play the field. What was his name again?

"Which brings us onto one last question. Who the hell is Jack Turner?"

# Framed

Mrs. Joy Hearty was far from joyful, and the only thing hearty about her looked to be her generous diet. She seemed less than pleased, standing in the doorway, staring blearily out at us through the smoke drifting up from the cigarette stuck to her bottom lip.

Next to me, Tompkins shifted his feet, probably trying to keep warm. I held up my badge, forcing the chatter from my voice, and resisted the urge to shout through the driving rain. "I'm Detective Inspector Ashcroft, Mrs. Hearty. This is Detective Constable Tompkins. Could we ask you and your husband a few questions?" I took the tiniest of steps towards the doorway, making sure she was clear the question-asking would take place inside, out of the freezing downpour.

She gave me a look I'd seen before many times — *interfering coppers* — like she'd just wiped me off her shoe. I glanced back at the safe warmth of the Ford Mondeo parked up the road. If she didn't let us in soon, it was going to be immaterial.

With the timing of a professional, Tompkins

sneezed, and she shifted her gaze to him, "Aye, you'd better come in then. Wipe yer feet." She walked back into the narrow, terraced house leaving the inviting doorway open.

Inside it was lovely and warm. A heat that was in stark contrast to the icy December rain. It quickly became stifling, even in my sodden state. She led us into the lounge, where we found Mr. Hearty, feet up, watching the rugby.

"Whatsit?" he grunted, barely glancing at his wife.

"Police."

I did the introductions again. He wasn't exactly welcoming either, but he did switch off the television and pull his vest more neatly across his beer belly.

"Amanda, go and put the kettle on." The teenage girl in the corner dragged herself to her feet, offered her mother a scowl and disappeared into the kitchen. The Hearty daughter was ill-placed in a household filled with her rotund parents—slim and pretty, set to be a real heartbreaker in a few years.

"What seems to be the problem, officers?" Fred Hearty had decided the business-like approach was best. He gestured to the two armchairs across from him. I displaced a copy of The Sun, and gladly rested my feet.

I let Tompkins do the talking initially. I directed my own attention to the subtler reactions; looking for any sign of lies or discomfort. So far, there was none. The Heartys, while hardly the pinnacle of civilisation, didn't seem like criminals.

"Mr. Hearty, we'd like to ask you a few questions regarding an incident that took place last Saturday. Would you mind telling us where you were between the hours of six p.m. and eight p.m.?" Tompkins did well; the question asked lightly, no sense of threat.

I could see him lining up his following statement, ready to catch Hearty off guard. *"Really? Then how is it that we have CCTV footage of you shooting a man in the head in a pawnshop in Palmers Green at precisely that time."*

Fred was a tougher customer than that though. "I was in bed in the Victoria Infirmary, recovering from having my appendix out." He stared unhelpfully at Tompkins and then lifted his vest to show off a bandage in the appropriate place. "Been stuck at home recovering all week."

"Er..."

I decided it was time to help the constable out. "You're absolutely sure about that? They'll confirm it if we ring the hospital, will they?"

I'd passed their cooperation boundary with that one. Fred was starting to get a bit edgy. "Course they bloody will. What's all this about anyway?"

I told them.

"Well, can't be. Like I said, I was in 'ospital. Bloody painful it was too. Emergency and all that.

Ruptured, it was."

I nodded, getting to my feet. "Yes, you're quite right. Obviously, no way it could be you, Mr. Hearty. I'm terribly sorry to have bothered you."

Tompkins gave me a look — *that's it*?

I nodded gently to him and stepped out into the hallway. "No need to see us out, we can find the way. Have a good afternoon, now."

It was still tipping down outside, so we waited until we'd hurried back to the car before resuming conversation.

"What was all that about, sir? It has to be him, I've seen the video myself."

I sighed. I'd had an odd feeling about this case as soon as we'd identified the man in the footage. "I agree, Tompkins. It certainly looks a lot like him, but it can't be him. You heard him, he was in hospital."

"And you believe him?"

"We'll check it out, of course. But it'd be a pretty damn stupid choice of alibi if he's lying." No, Fred Hearty wasn't my killer. There was more to this than met the eye.

"Take us back to the station, Adam. Then I want you to go up to the VI and check out his story. Take a photo. I want you to find someone who'll give you a positive ID; confirm it was definitely him up there."

"Sir."

"Oh, and check the birth records. Let's make sure

Fred Hearty doesn't have a twin brother lurking anywhere." I knew somehow he wouldn't, but best to cover all eventualities.

△△△

I sat with my feet on my desk, drying off, watching the security video from the pawnshop over and over, hoping to catch something I'd missed before.

The man looked extremely similar to Fred Hearty, even in the jumpy, black and white images of the film. He entered the shop, which was otherwise empty, and confronted the man behind the counter, soon-to-be-dead Alec Harmon. There was some heated debate, before he drew the revolver. At that point, Harmon closed up the shop, and the pair spent a good twenty minutes going through old security tapes at the back of the room, Hearty's double with the gun to the shop owner's back.

The screen of the small CCTV monitor they watched was just visible on the film, and I already had the lads in the lab trying to piece together which tape it was they watched last and what it was the man was after.

The whole thing was disjoint in my head. It didn't make sense. The actions of the shooter indicated a crime of passion, or revenge —

something wrapped in emotion. He'd shot a man in the head for something he'd done and made no effort to take the obvious step of destroying the tape of it afterwards. And yet, he'd sat calmly for over a quarter of an hour poring over videos, looking for something. But what? Then, to top the whole thing off, Fred Hearty, the man identified as the wielder of the gun by multiple people, had a stone-cold alibi for the time of death.

Alec Harmon wouldn't be missed. If he'd died in less confusing circumstances then he'd have hardly warranted my attention. A known thief, with a record as long as your arm, it had only been a matter of time before someone took serious offence to his method of obtaining stock.

Harmon had been dead a week. I'd been on the case four days and, so far, nothing but brick walls. I had feelers out though. Something would crop up eventually to give us all a hint.

△ △ △

Two days later we had our lead. The boys in the lab had gone through over a week of CCTV footage, comparing images, calculating tape lengths, tracking use of fast-forward and rewind, and had finally come up with what they thought was the last thing Alec Harmon saw before he died. The thing our Fred look-a-like had been searching for.

"Okay, roll it." The whole team was assembled in the briefing room, the video projected onto the wall.

The pawnshop appeared in the picture. Same jumpy, black and white images from the same camera. The timestamp in the corner indicated this was from three days before the murder. A woman, well dressed, mid-forties, entered the shop and spent a few minutes browsing, picking out a couple of items before taking her purchases to the counter. She bought a small microwave oven, and a metallic photo frame. Once she'd handed over her money, she left.

"That's it?" asked a voice from the back.

The technician shrugged, "So we think, yes."

I pondered it for a moment. Killing someone over a microwave seemed a bit excessive. Something hidden inside it maybe? Or was it the picture frame that was significant? It hardly looked expensive in the grainy images.

I stood up. "Right. I want to know who this woman is. Put her face on the TV if you need to. And see if there've been any robberies recently with anything similar to that microwave or photo frame reported missing." I left Tompkins to sort out the details of who did what and headed up to the DSU's office to give him a progress report.

△ △ △

A day and a half later, with pressure for progress from above mounting and still no nearer identifying the woman buying the microwave, I was pleased to be offered the chance of a different thread to pull.

A helpful member of the public had phoned in to say she'd recognised the man from the original footage we'd broadcast on the local news. We obviously had the (incorrect) Fred Hearty ID already, but she didn't have a name, just a location, and that piqued my interest.

"In the gym?"

"Oh yes, he was quite keen. There every night, working away on the treadmill."

Somehow Mr. Hearty didn't strike me as a regular gym-goer. Could this be his doppelganger? The real killer? "Could you give me the address of this gym?"

She did so. "Funny thing is, I didn't really put two and two together, with the video I mean, until he'd stopped coming."

"Stopped?" I asked, now even more confused about the whole thing.

"Yes, about three days ago I think. I've not seen him since. Odd, because like I said, he was in there every day for a month before that. Maybe one of those sponsored things, or something?"

I thanked the woman and decided I'd take a break and headed up to the gym to ask a few questions.

△△△

The ActiveU Fitness Centre was rather more upmarket than I'd been expecting. Situated at the top of a healthy rise, it offered pleasant views over fields and further towards the centre of London while you burned the calories. Again, this was the sort of place that was totally at odds with the impression I'd got of Fred Hearty in our brief encounter – I was even more convinced this lead might have merit.

I flashed my badge at the receptionist. She was all makeup and sweatbands but her welcoming smile wavered as she realised who I was. There was even a slight sideways glance as if looking for a colleague or supervisor for moral support. In the end she decided she was stuck with me, so the cheesy front-of-house mode came back with a vengeance.

"Welcome to ActiveU Health and Fitness! How can I help you today, officer?"

I got down to business. "I'm looking for a man who I believe has been frequenting this facility up until a few days ago." I described the suspect to her, trying to remember a few more details than 'fat' and 'middle-aged'.

"Oh yes! Rather gruff gentleman. Not very friendly at all." She frowned as she said this as if reprimanding a pet cat for clawing the furniture. "He used to come in at six o'clock sharp every night, but I've not seen him since Tuesday. Although, Wednesday's my day off."

I nodded, glancing at her nametag. 'Elli' was being rather more helpful than I'd expected from first impressions. I wondered if this was a holiday job on a break from a PhD in advanced hospitality. "And was he a member?"

"Oh yes. This is a private club. You can't get in if you're not a member." She gestured at the entry barriers and at that moment a patron came in and stuck his access card in the slot to open it by way of a helpful impromptu demonstration.

I asked her to check the system for Hearty's name first. This was accomplished with more grinning efficiency, but her face betrayed some confusion as the search results came up on the screen. "Hmm, no match. I guess it must have been someone else after all."

Hopefully, my killer. "Possibly. You said he came in at six each night. Does the system keep a record of who enters at what time?"

"Ooh! Good idea! Hang on..." More typing and searching later, we had our answer. "Here we go. I've run a search of entries from five fifty-five to five past six for the last two weeks. Looks like the man's been a bit naughty. The only match that consistently shows up is a Nick Mason. But that's not the same man!" She rotated her screen to show me a digital membership card with a picture of a much younger, fitter man. Not the man from the video. No resemblance to Fred Hearty.

I nodded slowly, pondering what on earth that meant.

"Do you think the card was stolen? Is that why you're here?" she asked. "I'd better tell my manager about this. You're not allowed to lend your card out."

"Yes, good idea. You've been very helpful. Oh, before I go, could you give me an address for Mr. Mason?"

Tompkins met me at Mason's flat, which was a rather flash affair in one of the new developments on the west side of town. Somehow, I wasn't expecting to find Nick Mason smiling and happy, missing one gym membership card that had been conveniently stolen a few weeks ago. This case was getting too strange for it to be anything that simple.

There was no response to the doorbell – no one home.

"No luck, sir," muttered Tompkins. "Do you want me to post a constable here in case he comes back?"

"Given this is a murder investigation, I'm a bit worried for Mr. Mason's safety. Let's see if we can find someone who will let us in." It was a stretch. I had nothing like enough evidence for a warrant. Only the loosest of circumstantial evidence linked Mason with the murder.

We tracked down the building supervisor, and, as

I'd hoped, he had a master key which opened all the apartments. He seemed convinced by our badges and concerned tones that it was acceptable to let us into Mason's place.

Inside the flat was smallish, but well kitted out. Living room and small kitchen alcove on one side, master bedroom on the other with a spotless bathroom in between.

Something was amiss about the place, and it took me a minute to put my finger on it. Appliances littered the place: large widescreen TV, but no DVD player; brand new oven and fitted hob, but no microwave; Playstation controller, but no Playstation.

"Looks like the place's been done over recently," commented Tompkins, voicing my own thoughts perfectly.

I nodded, "I wonder if Mr. Mason had a picture frame stolen at the same time." Things were falling into place somewhat, but I was still lacking significant proof of a connection. The hint of a recently stolen microwave oven was never going to be enough.

I moved to look in the bedroom. One of the walls was covered by a bookcase, the shelves stuffed with small plastic containers. They turned out to be memory cards; the sort used in cameras. I looked through a few of them, but they were just marked with numbers. I picked a few at random and handed them to Tompkins. “Let’s see what’s on these. Bring them back to the station.”

Of Mason himself, there was no sign. We left the place as we’d found it, less the borrowed items, and I arranged to have a constable keep watch in case Mason returned.

The whole case took a rather nasty turn when we saw what was on the memory cards.

Tompkins and I sat in my office staring at the computer monitor in the corner. Each of the cards were the same. They contained a series of video files each of which showed a fixed view of a bedroom. The bedrooms of teenaged girls who could be seen talking on the phone, dressing, undressing, studying, lounging about, and generally going about their lives.

“Bloody hell, he’s a Peeping Tom!” exclaimed Tompkins, stating the obvious. “High-tech at that. How’s he getting these images?”

“He must have planted cameras in their rooms,” I said, thinking out loud. “But how?” In the back of my mind the pieces were starting to come together, but I still couldn’t quite grasp the big picture.

A possible link fell into place at least. I turned back to Tompkins, “Send a team back to the Hearty’s. I want them to search the daughter’s bedroom for a hidden camera.”

He looked dubious. Hadn’t we ruled our Hearty’s involvement now? “If you want, sir.” I did.

There was a knock at the door and a constable stuck his head in. "We've ID'd the woman in the pawnshop video, sir."

△ △ △

We arranged to meet Helena Naysmith – the woman from the video – that evening. On the way over, I got a call confirming there had indeed been a tiny camera hidden in Amanda Hearty's bedroom. It was a cheap model with no ability to upload to the cloud, which meant Mason would have needed not only to stash it there in the first place, but visit again to get the contents of the memory cards. How had he managed that undetected across possibly hundreds of girls' rooms?

Tompkins was bemused. "How did you know? Are we thinking Hearty is involved in this after all?"

We'd checked the alibi and ruled out a twin brother. Still, a man matching Fred's description was somehow connected to Mason, who in turn had been spying on Hearty's daughter. Too many coincidences for my liking.

"Let's just keep following the evidence," I said to Tompkins. My gut was ahead of my brain on this one – I wasn't able to explain all my instincts just yet.

Marcus Naysmith was in fantastic shape for a man in his mid-forties. He didn't look at day over thirty. He beamed at us from the doorway. "Officers.

We've been expecting you. Do come in."

His wife had put on tea and biscuits in preparation for our visit. All very welcoming and nice. Helena Naysmith was quite a beauty and, like her husband, significantly younger-looking than the forty-three years our records indicated. She had not appeared so spry in the low-quality CCTV footage. My gut seemed keen to add this to the list of incongruous facts associated with the case.

As we'd called ahead, they knew what to expect, so we were able to sip our tea and munch on custard creams in great comfort while they talked. They told us they were terribly sorry about the pawnshop owner and that they had no idea the things they'd bought were stolen. We could have the microwave back if that was any help, although it was just the model they'd been looking for, which is why she'd gone into the pawnshop in the first place.

"The photo frame is a different story, I'm afraid. In the end I didn't quite like it as much once I'd got it out of the shop. You know how it is."

"So where is it now, ma'am?" I asked, cursing internally.

"My brother just got a promotion, so we sent it over to him as a little present to go in his new office," interjected Marcus.

This was turning into a wild goose chase. It was only some tenuous connections and my instincts that were justifying all this effort over a picture frame. I wasn't sure what it was I expected to find when we tracked it down. I just knew I'd not be happy until we closed off this line of enquiry.

We got Henry Naysmith's details from the couple and resolved to speak to him the next day. We also confiscated the microwave. The lab would check it properly, but from a cursory examination we couldn't see anything special about it, or evidence anything had been stashed inside. That left the picture frame as our only lead.

△△△

In the morning, I was surprised to spot Fred Hearty lingering in the station's reception area. I intercepted him.

"Mr. Hearty?"

He turned and gave me a blank look.

"It's DI Ashcroft. We met the other day?"

"Oh, right, of course. Sorry. Don't know where my head's at." He looked a bit more presentable than the other day, at least.

"That's all right. Were you after an update on the case involving your daughter?" I could imagine he and his wife were distraught at the realisation someone had been spying on their child.

"Uh, yeah. I guess so." He seemed a bit jumpy – probably police stations weren't on his list of usual haunts.

"Well, it's an ongoing case, so I can't tell you much, but, let me get you a cup of tea." I felt a bit sorry for him – a fish out of water.

I led him back to my office and got him a seat before going to grab a couple of teas from the refreshments stand. When I returned, he was standing up against the desk, peering over at the open files littering its surface. I quickly shuffled them out of the way and handed over the tea.

"Sorry, can't let you look at those! I can tell you we're doing everything we can to track down the man responsible for the cameras. We have some leads and I'm hopeful of a resolution soon." The standard non-specific spiel, albeit, I did feel like we genuinely had leads, even if they didn't all make sense yet.

He nodded. "Thanks. So, you think you're close to tracking down the suspect?"

"As ever, there are some things we don't quite understand yet, but I'm confident of some good progress over the next couple of days."

He downed the rest of the tea, which must have hurt – mine was still much too hot. "Thanks for your time, Inspector. I'll look forward to some news soon."

He walked out. I felt like something was off about him. I couldn't put my finger on what is was. Maybe the stress of the situation was taking its toll.

Once he'd left, I tracked down Tompkins. To avoid

making a liar out of myself, we needed start making sense of all this today.

Next on the agenda was our latest attempt to track down the elusive picture frame, which was supposedly now with the younger Naysmith brother. I'd been unable to catch him on the phone, so I sent Tompkins to his home address while I went to his office to maximise the chance of us getting hold of him.

I was successful. Henry Naysmith was doing well for himself. I was shown up to a large corner office with impressive views. I wasn't clear on what they did here – some sort of consultancy – but it paid well.

He shook my hand and gestured for me to sit. "What can I do for you, Inspector?"

He didn't seem to be expecting me, which suggested his brother had not forewarned him of the enquiry. "I'm trying to track down an item which I suspect is now in your possession. A small metallic photograph frame. I'm led to believe your brother sent it to you as a present."

He frowned. "Marcus? Did he? If so, I'm afraid I've not received it yet. Do you know when he sent it?"

Damn. With his expensive suit and big salary, Naysmith was probably used to high-pressure situations, but he seemed unruffled and calm. I didn't have the sense he was lying. "That's a shame.

It was sent only in the last couple of days, so is probably still in transit." I slid my card across the desk. "Can I ask you to give me a call as soon as it arrives? It's related to an important investigation."

"Of course, I'll be sure to call you as soon as I get it. I left home quite early today, so it might even be waiting for me when I get back this evening." He smiled. "To be honest, I'm curious as to why Marcus thought it would make a good present. I'm something of a confirmed bachelor. Framed photos aren't really my thing! I think the only one I have is of my poor old cat – he passed away last year."

I didn't need his life story. "I'm sorry to hear that. Thank you for the help. You can call any time." A sad reflection of my own social life, but true. Once I was buried in a case, I found it hard to focus on much else.

△△△

With no other leads, there was nothing to do now but wait to hear from Henry Naysmith. I took the opportunity to finish up some paperwork, so it wasn't until nearly the end of the day that I caught up with Tompkins.

"Sorry I didn't find your earlier, sir, but Naysmith didn't know anything about the frame. I reckon it might still be in the post."

I frowned. "Yes, I know that. How do *you* know

that?" The only place that information was recorded was in the notebook on my desk. I'd told no one.

His turn to look perplexed. "I talked to him outside his house earlier. You sent me there!"

"You saw him? What time?"

I think Tompkins was starting to doubt my sanity by this point. Some of the angles I'd found worthy of exploration were, admittedly, a little left-field. Maybe he was right.

"About ten thirty. I just caught him on his way out." The same time I'd talked to him at his office. Which was impossible.

"You're absolutely sure?"

"Sir, yes!" He seemed exasperated. "Look, do you think we might be putting too much focus on this picture frame? Maybe we should look more into Hearty – we could have missed something. The evidence linking the frame to things is just too thin!"

*Too thin.* The realisation hit me hard as all the various strands in my head finally started to pull together. That's what was wrong with Fred Hearty when he visited me this morning. He was too thin. Not the sort of thin that came from being a bit gaunt through stress, rather the sort that comes from a month of regular gym visits. Not Fred Hearty at all. The killer. And I'd left him in my office with the case files.

"Adam, I've made a terrible mistake! We need to

get to Henry Naysmith's house right now. He's in danger! Call some backup and meet me at the car."

Tompkins didn't need telling twice. He may have had his doubts, but he knew from the tone of my voice I wasn't messing around now. He raced into action.

Soon we were on our way to Naysmith's luxury country retreat just beyond the outskirts of town. I knew how it all fitted together now. I couldn't explain how it was possible, but that was a secondary concern.

Initially, the existence of Fred Hearty's double could have just been a confusing coincidence. Now, I'd seen him with my own eyes. Not a man who happened to resemble Hearty approximately, but an identical man (ignoring the weight loss). Identical to the extent it hadn't even occurred to me it wasn't Fred Hearty I'd spoken to in my office.

Add to that the emergence of a second doppelganger – with Tompkins and I both interviewing Naysmith at the same time – and we had proof something bizarre was going on.

"So, you know who the killer is then, sir?" asked Tompkins as we raced too fast down country roads.

"Yes. It's Nick Mason." I was sure. Proving any of this was going to be a challenge though.

Tompkins was sceptical. "The killer didn't look anything like Mason," he protested.

"It was a disguise. He was disguised as Fred

Hearty."

"What? Why?" he asked.

"Because it's easy to get access to Amanda Hearty's bedroom to install a camera if you look like her dad."

"What's that got to do with the murder? Or Naysmith?" He sounded bewildered.

"When you thought you spoke to Naysmith this morning, you didn't. It was Mason – disguised again."

"He looked exactly like his photo, sir. It didn't look at all like he was wearing a disguise. Nor did Hearty in that video for that matter. I mean, it just doesn't seem likely."

Mason had gone to Naysmith's house for one purpose – to intercept the photo frame's delivery. I'd inadvertently given him the address by letting him see the files in my office. Tompkins had reached the house shortly afterwards and unsuspectingly interviewed a man who looked just like Henry Naysmith. As my gut had been telling me all along, the photo frame was the key. How it worked, I had no clue. What it could do was now clear.

"I agree, but nonetheless I think it's the case. You just have to accept that Mason had a way to disguise himself perfectly as someone else, and everything slots into place."

Poor Tompkins frowned. He was now trying to make sense of several impossible things at once.

Fortunately, we were nearly at Naysmith's place, so I could stop trying to explain the unexplainable – it was time for action.

I got on the radio to the other cars: "Sirens and lights on as we approach." I was pretty sure I knew what Mason's next move was and his plan would only work if he was undiscovered. If you can step into the shoes of a rich bachelor like Henry Naysmith, you might decide those shoes could be comfortable long term. Especially if you'd just spent a month stuck looking like fat, middle-aged Fred Hearty while you tracked down the precious item stolen from your flat. By contrast Naysmith was a massive upgrade. You could only steal someone's life, however, if you disposed of them in secret. I prayed we weren't too late. I prayed I wasn't wrong.

The train of police cars raced up the wide driveway, sirens blaring, blue lights casting strange shadows. The cars slid to a halt in front of the impressive modern building Henry Naysmith called home. The tactical officers ran up to the door and breached it. Tompkins and I hung back until it was safe.

Several shouts of "Clear!" and we were allowed to go up and enter the house. Naysmith was sprawled in the hallway. He'd been hit from behind as he entered the house. The good news was he was alive. We'd got there in time. An ambulance was on its way.

That also meant the killer couldn't be far. The tactical team leader came up to me. "House is empty, sir. We've scouted around the grounds too. No sign of anyone else. Doors are all locked from the inside, so we're not sure where he could have gone. Must have scarpered before we got here, I guess."

It made no sense. Mason was not intending to leave here at all. Running before we arrived didn't add up, especially with Naysmith alive. We must have startled him, and he'd panicked and run into the house, finding his escape routes locked. He had to be here.

I walked into the kitchen. There on the counter-top were not one but two photo frames. A wooden frame which was empty, a photo of Henry Naysmith discarded beside it. The other one – the metallic one from the pawnshop – held a picture of the deceased cat Naysmith had told me about. Obviously swapped into the metal frame out of its original wooden one.

The cat in the picture looked identical to the non-dead one cowering in the corner of the room, glaring at me.

Tompkins joined me. "I guess Mason's in the wind, sir. Sorry we missed him."

I glanced at the kitty and smiled. I picked up the picture frame and slid it into an evidence bag. "I suppose you're right. Somehow, I doubt he'll be causing any more trouble though. I have the feeling he may have made a rash decision in his panic to escape. Do me a favour and give veterinary services a call." I stared at the cat. "That animal belongs in a cage."

I turned and headed back towards the car. Who knew what that photo frame really was – advanced technology stolen from some secret lab maybe? Regardless, this outcome was for the best. I hadn't been looking forward to submitting a report with the words *magic picture frame* in it one little bit.

# In Ted We Trust

Time is starting to run out now, I can tell. They won't tell us exactly how long is left. Rumours suggest it could be as little as six months.

Doctor Lufnitz calls quiet as he climbs up to the podium to give us all the weekly status update. He looks old. Much older than he did a few months back. He surveys the two hundred expectant faces crammed into the meeting room. Will there be good news today? I doubt it. Anything significant would have leaked out by now. We're all working toward the same goal, after all.

The tired way he assembles his papers before addressing us, eyes downcast, tells the story immediately.

"After last month's great success in stabilising the large wormhole, I'm afraid to say progress has continued to be slow over the last week." There are sighs and mutters from the gathered masses as if they didn't know that was coming. "Nonetheless, we have moved forward. The matter stream group has succeeded in passing a solid object through the small wormhole in the lab environment." Success! But he raises a hand and kills the cheers with the bad news. "However, all attempts to pass living tissue through the wormhole are still failing. In parallel, the destination search group has started work analysing the data we have gathered and continue to gather. There's a lot to get through, obviously."

I sigh. He's not kidding. The information on my plate to sift through is three years' work already and more comes in every day. With more than a hundred others doing the same thing, the amount of data is astronomical. Even if we could look through it all, there's no guarantee we'd find what we're looking for: that elusive escape route.

"Get Lucky Ted on the case!" calls a voice from the back, eliciting laughter. Ted looks embarrassed, lowering his head and forcing a weak smile. I bet he almost wishes he'd never made the suggestion that allowed us to stabilise the large wormhole. The limelight doesn't suit him, but we're all grateful. It was starting to look hopeless.

As I leave the meeting, heading back to my terminal to stare at yet more data from the wormhole probes, the mood of my colleagues around me is low. We got lucky last month, but there are still seemingly insurmountable problems to be conquered and no time to do it.

We're not the only project, of course. There are hundreds of others, trying a huge range of different techniques, based in locations scattered around the globe. I'm starting to hope there'll be good news from one of them soon. It looks as though we're going to fall short.

By lunch, the mood has picked up again. It always happens this way. If it didn't, I think we'd all just go home and get drunk. There's a great level of group determination among us: we can beat this thing!

We sit together and eat our sandwiches, taking time out to talk about lighter topics. All except Ted. He sits alone in the corner, as always, munching his sandwich and sharing the morning's events with his late wife, a picture of whom is glued inside the lid of his lunchbox. It's his little ritual each day. We all know better than to disturb him.

The week passes much as the last. The work is dull, but with such high stakes no one slacks off, everyone applies the whole of their PhD-adorned brains to the problem. Somewhere in this mass of data is a new home.

I arrive late the following Monday, and I can tell there's some sort of commotion. I hurry into the common room and ask what's going on.

"They passed a live mouse through the small wormhole this morning. You'll never guess who solved the problem! It was Ted!"

I state my disbelief: he doesn't even work on that part of the project. Apparently, there was a misdelivered parcel and, while picking it up, Ted slipped and sat on a control panel. Of all the things! He really is Lucky Ted! There are plans to take him out for a slap-up lunch to celebrate, but he declines. He's got his lunch already, thank you. Everyone understands: there's someone else he'd rather spend his break with.

The building is euphoric for a couple of days. We're close now, surely. Two weeks later, however, things are looking no better and it's hard to see how we can analyse all the data in time. Doctor Lufnitz looks drained and depressed as he gives the status update. I feel there's a hint of panic creeping into everyone.

On the way home, late one night, I find myself in the lift with Sarah. I know her vaguely; she's on the same team as I am: a new face, fresh from university. I feel a bit sorry for her. She's had no time to live. Working fourteen-hour days, seven days a week is no fun when you should be out partying.

She turns to me. We're alone and there's a second of awkwardness as the silence drifts on for too long. "David?" I turn and smile, discomfort lifting. "I don't want to die a virgin."

I almost choke. She ignores my reaction. "I like you. You're nice. Take me home. Please."

There is the first crack. Civilised society, held together by threads of bravado and professionalism, starts to come apart with a proposition from a cute blonde. A woman I doubt would give me the time of day under normal circumstances. I feel it too. It's that slight panic in the pit of your stomach; the fear you're trying to ignore as it screams at you to enjoy your final days.

I reach out and with a smile I take her hand. We walk calmly back to my apartment. No words are required, not now. Tomorrow, maybe things will be the same, or maybe the world will have changed as more cracks appear. For now, it doesn't matter.

We don't speak at all until after we've made love. She more than makes up with enthusiasm what she lacks in experience, and I realise it was definitely something I needed.

Finally, lying back on the sheets, still naked, she turns to me. "Do you think it'll hurt when the meteor hits?"

I've no more idea of the answer to her question than she does. There are lots of unknowns. I tell her it won't and stroke her hair, but I'm afraid now. I think it will hurt. I think it will hurt a lot.

The next day, there are more cracks: several people don't show up for work, and the news reports rioting in South America. Sarah and I eat lunch together. Ted is there in the corner.

"Do you think she's an angel?" asks Sarah out of the blue. I give her an odd look. Who does she mean? "Well, you know, he's always talking to his wife, and then he keeps being the one to help make the next breakthrough on the project. I just wondered if maybe his wife is an angel. She's looking out for us all."

I smile and shrug. I admit it's possible. If so, she'd better hurry up and help us find a suitable destination. There's no time left. Evacuating the entire population of a planet is going to take a while.

Somehow Sarah's thoughts seem to get around and over the next couple of weeks Ted is no longer Lucky, but Angelic Ted. There are more empty seats now, and the news is full of anarchy. It's the end, and time has run out.

I consider taking Sarah and running away: make best use of the last few weeks. But inside me there's still a glimmer of hope. A resolve in my spirit that refuses to give up. I stay at my desk.

Doctor Lufnitz himself is sorting data now, filling in for those who have done what I cannot. He looks like an old man, slumped in his chair. How frustrating for his dream to be almost a salvation, only to be stopped at the final hurdle.

Wednesday morning, I arrive to find the entire building surrounded by armed soldiers. It takes several checks before I'm allowed in. Sarah bounds up to me as soon as she sees me. She looks happier and more vibrant than I've ever seen and hope surges upwards. Is there good news?

"Ted did it!" she cries. There are tears in her eyes. Ted. It had to be, somehow. Divine inspiration? Perhaps. I don't care about the how, just the what.

The planet Ted has found lurking in the data is far from a paradise, but it has the right atmosphere and is likely inhabitable. We did it, and there's still time. Just.

From now on, we're bystanders as the military take the operation over. We monitor the wormhole and keep it stable as the initial manned probes are sent through to survey the world that must be humanity's new home. Elsewhere, a huge global effort begins to transport everyone here to the mouth of the wormhole. Everyone. Seven billion people. It's mind-blowing, and it's going to be tight. We can get everyone off, but it's all a desperate rush.

The next weeks are a blur. The initial probes have come back and confirmed the world is habitable. It's a cold, rocky wasteland, and, so far, there's not much evidence of natural resources. Nonetheless, it's a whole lot better than the alternative.

I'm busy helping the team to make sure we get people and equipment through the wormhole as efficiently as possible. The mood is lifted one morning when I'm handed a t-shirt on my way in and I have to chuckle at its logo: "In Ted We Trust!" Soon all the technical people are wearing them. Even Doctor Lufnitz. Not Ted though; he's too embarrassed. He also refuses all suggestions that we try to get the new Earth named "Planet Ted".

By the time the meteor is visible in the night sky — a bright and imposing new star — we're almost done. With an impossible effort the entire planet has been raided of its population and a good proportion of its livestock, and the world is coming to terms with a far harsher existence a thousand light-years away. It will be hard, but we'll make it. I almost gave up hope. Now a whole new world of possibilities exists. I take Sarah's hand as we ready ourselves to go through; our team is the last. I wave to Ted and ask him if he's coming. He'll just be a few minutes he says. One last thing to do. We understand and turn to walk towards a future of new opportunities.

△ △ △

Ted strolls slowly to his locker. The last man on Earth. He pulls out his lunchbox and walks to the canteen, sitting in his usual spot in the corner. He takes a deep breath, savouring the silence and emptiness.

He opens the lunchbox and pulls back the picture of the woman he cut from a magazine, revealing a single red button. He presses it and, after a moment, there is a connection.

He smiles. "We can stop the meteor now. They've all gone."

24977101R00099

Printed in Great Britain
by Amazon